"Now is the time

Angie gave Cole a mind?"

"Something like this." ...red his head and claimed her mouth with his.

Cole knew he was playing with fire. He was only going to graze her lips. But he found that he couldn't pull away. He needed another kiss and then another. He traced her full, soft lips with the tip of his tongue.

Angie opened her mouth and drew him in. Triumph swept through him. He cupped her jaw with both hands and tilted her head. She kissed him as if she couldn't get enough of him. Excitement pulsed through Cole as she grabbed his shirt and pulled him closer.

Cole wrenched away from Angie. Damn it, he thought, as he gulped in air. He forgot. He forgot where they were and why they were kissing.

Most of all, he forgot that kissing Angie was like sharing a piece of his soul....

Dear Reader,

My twin sister once told me that getting back with your ex is a lot like jump-starting your diet. After a few days you remember why it didn't work the first time. No matter how many stories you've heard about disastrous reunions, it's a tantalizing idea to have another chance with the one that got away. How would you act if you got a do-over?

Angie gets the opportunity in *The Bridesmaid's Best Man.* She's not over Cole and now she must pretend that they have rekindled their red-hot romance. This fake reunion is starting to feel a little too real and Angie discovers that their fling is even wilder the second time around.

Thanks for reading Angie and Cole's story. Don't forget to visit my website, susannacarr.com, for news, excerpts, contests and more.

Enjoy!

Susanna Carr

The Bridesmaid's Best Man

—

Susanna Carr

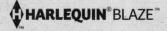

Recycling programs
for this product may
not exist in your area.

ISBN-13: 978-0-373-79773-8

THE BRIDESMAID'S BEST MAN

Copyright © 2013 by Jasmine Communications, LLC

Printed in U.S.A.

www.Harlequin.com

ABOUT THE AUTHOR

Susanna Carr lives in the Pacific Northwest with her family. When she isn't writing, Susanna enjoys reading romance and connecting with readers online. Visit her website, susannacarr.com.

Books by Susanna Carr

HARLEQUIN BLAZE

692—SUDDENLY SEXY

Did you know Susanna's titles
are also available as ebooks?
Visit www.Harlequin.com

To get the inside scoop on Harlequin Blaze and its talented writers, be sure to check out blazeauthors.com.

Other titles by this author available in ebook format. Don't miss any of our special offers. Write to us at the following address for information on our newest releases.

Harlequin Reader Service
U.S.: 3010 Walden Ave., P.O. Box 1325, Buffalo, NY 14269
Canadian: P.O. Box 609, Fort Erie, Ont. L2A 5X3

To Kathryn Lye, with thanks

1

THE DANCE MUSIC pulsed through the floor and the lights flashed across the shadowy room. As the bare-chested men danced for the screaming women, Angie Lawson glanced at her cell phone to check the time. How much longer was she required to be at this bachelorette party?

She jumped when she felt someone tap her on the shoulder. Angie whirled around and saw the bride-to-be behind her. Brittany was dressed to attract attention from her fire-engine-red bandage dress to the rhinestone tiara and veil perched on top of her long, coppery hair.

"Angie, you are supposed to be having fun." Brittany's whine seemed to pierce through the music. Her hands were on her hips and she tapped her foot impatiently. "You're my bridesmaid. It's practically required!"

Angie stared at her and then looked at the women standing on the table and chairs as they screamed for the well-endowed Tiger to take it all off. She returned her attention to Brittany. "This is what you notice?"

"And what *are* you wearing?" She gestured to Angie and gave a look of disgust. "It's a bachelorette party."

"There are half-naked men everywhere," she reminded the bride-to-be. "I didn't realize there would be a dress code."

"Absolutely, it is *my* party." Brittany flattened her manicured hand to her chest. "I am a personal shopper for an exclusive clientele and they're here."

Exclusive? Angie wanted to snort at the word. She had worked with some of the most accomplished and talented women in the Seattle area. The women here at Brittany's invitation were sloppy drunk and out of control. She was pretty sure one of them had tried to bite a stripper.

"Not only do I have to look good," Brittany said, "but so do my bridesmaids."

Angie glanced down at her clothes. She wore a glittery black tank, dark skinny jeans and—with great reluctance but her mother had insisted—strappy heels. There was nothing strange or offensive about her outfit.

She scanned the room, taking note of the other women in the upscale strip club that had been reserved for Brittany's bachelorette party. The guests were not like the flannel-shirt, thick-framed-eyeglasses and designer-boots crowd she knew. They weren't even the yoga-pants and organic-coffee group from the suburbs. The women wore flirty dresses and skintight miniskirts. The outfits were wild and sexy.

Oh. Those were two words that wouldn't describe her. Ever. Angie sighed and fought the urge to hunch her shoulders. Once again, she had dressed all wrong. She thought what she had worn was sophisticated and trendy enough that she would blend in. Instead she looked like a dark giant among the sugarplum fairies.

"I mean, really, Angie." She tossed her hands up with frustration. "What's wrong with showing a little cleavage?"

Now Brittany was really beginning to sound just like her mother. "Nothing." Angie shrugged. And it was a good thing she felt that way, since she was going to flash the whole world when she wore her bridesmaid dress. It was tight, shiny and barely covered the essentials.

"I give up. Just try to look like you're enjoying yourself," Brittany said as she marched off.

Angie froze at those parting words. She had made a valiant effort to get into a party mood but she was bored. And that was cause for worry. Actually, she hadn't been interested in any man since Cole walked out of her life. That was months ago and yet, watching these gorgeous men had left her cold. Why couldn't she enjoy watching a man dance? It didn't make sense. She was young and healthy. What was wrong with her?

"Don't listen to Britt."

Angie peered down and saw Brittany's assistant at her side. Cheryl, a petite and curvy blonde who usually wore jeans and animal-print tops, was dressed in a leopard-print tube dress and skyscraper heels.

"She gives unsolicited fashion advice all the time," Cheryl said with a weary smile. "She doesn't mean anything by it."

"It's okay. It doesn't bother me," Angie assured Cheryl, but the woman was already trailing her boss.

And it didn't bother her that much. She heard the complaint so many times that it had become white noise. Boyfriends had always wanted her to wear revealing clothes and well-intentioned friends kept trying to give her a makeover. No matter how much they insisted, she wouldn't give in. She knew she would never meet their expectations. What would be the point of trying?

She had learned to resist this type of help from a young age. Her mother used to make her go on shopping expeditions that felt more like death marches. Despite her mother's perseverance to create a girly look for Angie, it never stuck. Angie preferred the hand-me-downs from her brothers rather than the ruffled dresses and makeup.

But maybe she had gone too far. Her mother thought Cole had lost interest because Angie didn't work hard enough on her appearance. Her friends weren't quick to shoot down the idea, either.

She didn't want to believe it. When they had first met at a gym, Angie hadn't been dressed to impress. She had been sweaty and in desperate need of a shower after an intense workout. And yet Cole couldn't stop flirting with her.

Even after that Cole never asked her to dress up and he didn't make any complaints about her customary ponytail or lack of pretty lingerie. He didn't suggest that she needed to wear tight clothes to reveal the hard work she put in exercising. He thought she was strong and sexy.

But maybe she hadn't been sexy enough....

"Angie!"

Angie cringed when she recognized the maid of honor's voice. She looked for an escape route but she was stuck unless she wanted to get on stage with the strippers. That wasn't going to happen. Angie sighed with defeat and watched Heidi approach.

Heidi was tall, rail-thin and her short dark hair made the most of her dramatic features. Her blue one-shoulder dress and stiletto heels would have gotten Brittany's stamp of approval. Just being near Heidi made Angie feel drab and frumpy. The only thing they had in common was the gold bracelet they had received as a bridesmaid gift.

"You need to keep me away from Robin," Heidi declared.

Angie wondered where it was written in the brides-maid handbook that she had to be the referee? Heidi and Robin might be Brittany's sorority sisters but they hated each other. It was as if they were in competition over who was Brittany's favorite. Why anyone would spend energy on that was beyond Angie's imagina-tion. And from what Angie could tell, Brittany seemed to genuinely enjoy pitting the two against each other.

Unfortunately, she wasn't surprised by this side of Brittany and wished for the millionth time that she had found a good excuse to get out of being a brides-maid. But Patrick was the groom and her best friend since kindergarten. It was important to him that she was part of his wedding.

"I couldn't stand her in college," Heidi continued. "And she's even worse now."

"I admire your restraint," Angie deadpanned. "You're really doing everything you can to keep the drama out of Brittany's bachelorette party. That's a true friend."

"I know, right? I couldn't believe that Robin said the bridesmaid dresses are tacky. How could she say that? I love Britt's sense of style. I think the dresses are sexy and colorful."

Colorful? Angie bit down on her lip. Bile-green was a color, so Heidi was technically correct.

"And you can wear them again," Heidi informed her.

Angie nodded slowly. "Sure." But why would she want to go somewhere that required her to wear a bustier dress?

"Of course, Robin can't let anything other than designer touch her skin." Heidi crossed her arms and looked over her shoulder. "I think she's just bitter because the dress didn't come in vanity sizes. Her dress size is in double digits."

Angie gritted her teeth. This was exactly why she preferred hanging out with the guys. She was tempted to put Heidi in a headlock and tell her to grow up. It always worked on Patrick but she had a feeling it would cause a meltdown for Heidi.

The strip club plunged into darkness and the spotlight zeroed in on Brittany. "Oh," Heidi squealed as the DJ asked the bride-to-be to go on stage, "the strippers are going to give a special dance for Brittany. Go find a seat."

Angie watched Heidi run to the edge of the stage, teetering dangerously on her silver stilettos. She took a deep breath. So what if she wore the wrong clothes? Who cared if she was too shy to grope a man? It didn't mean she was sexually repressed, right? She could smile, clap and make sure everyone was having a good time. She was going to have fun tonight even if it killed her.

"What did she say about me?"

Angie jumped as Robin stood beside her. The woman's orange beaded halter dress was so short that at first Angie thought it was meant to be a shirt. "Heidi? She said the strippers were going to dance for Brittany."

"She was talking about me, wasn't she?" Her sleek black ponytail bobbed as she nodded her head.

"No," Angie lied.

Robin arched a perfectly groomed eyebrow. "She's just mad because Britt loved the bridal party spa and that was my idea. We all needed it, don't you think?"

Going to the spa had been a new experience for Angie. She had felt awkward in the hushed and ultra-feminine surroundings. The moment she had walked through the ornate doors, she had felt like a clumsy duck next to elegant swans. "You know, that was the first time I've been to a spa."

"No need to tell me that. I've seen your cuticles," Robin said. "But still, that event was designed to help the bride relax. And Britt has been incredibly stressed out."

Angie wholeheartedly agreed with that. Brittany had a strong vision for the wedding and reception, but there were too many details to keep track of. Even with her highly efficient assistant and three bridesmaids at her beck and call, there had been a series of problems to solve. "Maybe if she started eating."

"Don't even say that!" Robin shook her head vigorously. "Not until after the wedding. She has to fit into that dress."

No solid foods for a week? It sounded like torture to Angie. "The dress fits perfectly. She doesn't have anything to worry about. But she should stop the liquid diet. It can make a person tired and irritable."

Robin's eyes widened. "You think Britt is irritating?"

She really needed to be more careful with her words. Didn't she know by now that the bridal party was a walking, talking minefield? All the competition, insecurities and petty jealousies. Angie already had a sneaky suspicion that being Brittany's bridesmaid wasn't going to strengthen their relationship. She needed to work harder if she wanted to stay friends with Patrick. "No, I said—"

The hot pink stage curtains were ripped back and five strippers stood silently on the dark stage. They wore black neckties and low-slung leather pants. Angie jumped, startled, as the women around her went wild.

Robin raised her arms and whooped with delight as the first few notes of "It's Raining Men" played. Angie dutifully smiled and clapped as she watched the men start their routine around Brittany. The audacious choreography and frenetic lighting hid the fact that only a few were good dancers.

Angie's mouth dropped when she saw Brittany eagerly lay on the stage as one of the strippers straddled her. No one could accuse the bride-to-be of being shy. Brittany enjoyed the special attention.

The men had lean, athletic builds. Angie admired the hard abs and strong arms. She knew the work they had to put into getting sculpted bodies. They were attractive. Sexy. But she didn't feel the need to go crazy at the sight of them.

Perhaps it was because she worked as a personal trainer and was surrounded by muscular men every day. Or it could be that she felt self-conscious having a man gyrate in her face until she stuffed money in his sequined thong.

Or it could be none of those reasons. It could be that she wasn't acting as assertive and enthusiastic as the other women because she couldn't let go of her inhibitions. She tried that before. She had felt safe when she was with Cole. She knew she could be as outrageous and as daring as she wanted. She'd played out her deepest, darkest fantasies with him.

And then he dumped her. She was hurt and humiliated. Was she more mild than wild? Was she unable to compete with other women? She was afraid of the answer and had kept the sensual side of herself under wraps ever since.

Angie looked away from the stage as the knot in her stomach tightened and a flush of embarrassment crept up her neck. Not only had she felt safe with Cole, but at the same time, she'd also felt wild. She found it weird. No other man made her feel that way.

But she didn't want to think about that. She couldn't. It was better to accept that she didn't have a sensual side and move on. One day she'd regain her confidence. However, she wasn't going to lower her guard here, and definitely not with a stranger. It would be with someone she loved and trusted.

"Aren't these guys hot?" Robin yelled over the music.

"They are." Angie continued to clap to the beat as Brittany got to her feet and danced with the strippers. Some of her moves were downright dirty.

Robin elbowed her. "The bridesmaids get the next lap dances."

Angie lurched forward and her stomach twisted violently. "Up there on stage?"

"No, that honor is reserved for the bride. But you better pick one before Heidi grabs them all. Which one do you want?"

"Oh...it doesn't matter." She knew what would happen. The more audacious the dancer, the more uptight she would be. She was going to be laughed at for her discomfort. She wanted to refuse the dance but she had to act like a team player. She studied the men on stage, hoping to find one who understood personal space and boundaries.

"I can't decide between the guy groping Brittany or the one in the back."

Angie looked at where Robin pointed. The guy reminded her of Cole, from his short black hair to his solid, muscular build. She felt a surprising flutter of interest as her gaze traveled down his smooth chest, defined abs and lean hips. He had power and grace. He looked a lot like Cole. In fact—

She gasped and dragged her gaze to the man's face. She recognized the square jaw and full lips. The high cheekbones and strong nose. The short dark hair that felt soft to the touch. "No...way."

"What?" Robin asked. "Are you okay? What's wrong?"

Angie slumped into the nearest chair. She felt hot and cold from the shock but she continued to stare at Cole Foster from across the room. Her ex-boyfriend was on his hands and knees as he sinuously rolled his hips.

"Where the hell did he learn how to move like that?" She realized she had said it aloud and pressed her lips together.

"Who?" Robin asked. "The stripper? Do you know him?"

"No. I don't know him at all." She had shared intimate moments with this man. Loved him with her body and soul. Once she had bared it all to him, but it had been a mistake. It turned out she wasn't enough for Cole. And now she saw the truth with her own eyes as he stood on stage, performing for a group of panting women. "I thought he looked like someone I used to date."

Robin gave a bark of laughter. "Yeah, right. You dating a stripper."

"Stranger things have been known to happen," Angie murmured. Like Cole *becoming* a stripper. It didn't make sense. When she dated him, Cole had been a detective on the police force. And a good one at that.

Angie watched, stunned and openmouthed, as Cole ripped off his necktie and wrapped it around Brittany's waist, pulling the bride-to-be closer as the group of women screamed louder and reached for him.

Angie crossed her arms and sat stiffly in her chair. She wanted to disappear into the shadows. Leave before Cole saw her. She felt confused. Stupid. Territorial.

She felt betrayed and that didn't make any sense. At one time, this guy had made her feel special. Now it looked as if he knew how to make every woman feel that way. She wasn't dating Cole anymore and it didn't matter what he did. So why did she feel angry?

Cole turned his head and his gaze snagged hers. Angie's breath hitched in her throat as she stared into his blue eyes. He didn't look surprised to see her. It was as if he had known she was here all along.

She saw the determination flash across his face. *Uh-oh.* She knew that look. Angie wanted to leap from her seat but instead she braced herself. Her eyes widened with horror when she watched Cole jump from the stage. The women grabbed at him but he didn't pay them any attention as he strode straight for her.

These women were animals. Cole Foster tugged his leg away from a woman's fierce grip and ignored the fistful of dollars that another waved in his face. He'd never felt like a piece of meat until tonight. The crowd was rabid and ready to rip off his clothes.

He was having a difficult time focusing on his case and that wasn't like him. He was committed to this job—his real job—and prided himself on his profes-sionalism. Yet all he could think about was Angie sit-ting in the back row.

She hasn't changed a bit, Cole realized. Angie Law-son was strong, athletic and a natural beauty. Her wavy black hair was pulled back in a casual ponytail and she wore no makeup. She didn't need to. She had a healthy glow and vibrant energy that a person couldn't get in a bottle.

He noticed she wore a black tank top and jeans. He saw the strappy heels and knew that had to be her mother's interference. Angie dressed to hide or blend into the crowd. But she couldn't hide from him. He was always aware of her and nothing would ever change that.

It wasn't his plan to blatantly approach her. It could risk his assignment but he saw her rigid stance and crossed arms. Her eyes were wide and her mouth was tight with anger. Cole knew she was trying to hold it all in but she was about to blow his cover.

Maybe he should have given her an early warn-ing. He knew she would be here, he had been track-ing the bridal party for the past week. But he hadn't been able to determine how close Angie was with the other bridesmaids.

He stood before her, his heart beating fast, his skin slick with sweat. The leather pants clung to his legs and rode low on his waist. Angie was doing her best to keep her gaze somewhere around his ear.

She didn't say anything. There were a lot of things he wanted to say to her. Things like "Sorry," or "You're better off without me." Instead he said, "You're next."

Her eyes glittered with anger and she held out her hand to stop him. "No, thanks."

"Angie, what are you saying?" The woman he knew as Robin tapped her on the shoulder. "You just told me he looked like your ex. Go for it."

He got here in the nick of time. What else did she say about him? "I insist," he said with a hint of warning. "Bridesmaids are next in line."

She jutted out her chin. "How did you know that I'm a bridesmaid?"

"I was told ahead of time," he replied. He loved the sound of her voice. It was low, rough and sexy. He remembered it at the most inconvenient times.

Angie glared at him with suspicion. She crossed her legs and held her arms tighter around her. "Sorry, I don't have any dollar bills."

"Didn't you know you were coming to a strip club?"

"Don't mind her," Robin said. "She's new at this."

He leaned forward and rested his hands on the top of her chair. He caged her in and she pressed her spine against the back. Cole inhaled her scent and the memories bombarded him. "No money at all?" he asked.

"Not unless you want coins."

Cole's smile grew wide. He looked at Robin. "Tiger told the rest of us that he wants to be the one to give you the lap dance."

"See ya!" Robin blurted and raced to the stage, leaving them alone.

"There was no reason to send her away," Angie said and her words vanished as he straddled her legs. She immediately tensed up. "What are you doing?"

"This is the only way I can talk to you here," he said, but his mind was elsewhere. He was painfully aroused being this close to Angie. How was he going to put two words together while he was touching her? "Don't worry, I'll be gentle."

For some reason his assurance was met with a frosty stare. He watched with fascination as Angie's skin flushed red. "Don't worry about me," she said in a clipped tone. "Give me all that you've got."

"Angie, I know you're uncomfortable with all this." He saw the flash of injured pride in her eyes and he fell silent. Everything he said was being taken the wrong way.

"No, no, Cole. I'm curious. I've already seen some of your new moves. I didn't realize that you had been holding back with me."

"Holding back?" He never held anything back with Angie. Well, not physically.

"Go ahead, Cole." Angie leaned back in her chair. "Drive me wild."

2

COLE DIPPED HIS head and Angie closed her eyes. It was a defensive move but it didn't help. She could still feel the heat from his body. She licked her lips, remembering how his skin tasted. Warm and masculine.

"I need to talk to you," he said against her ear.

She felt his breath against her skin and shivered. "Apparently so. You've gone through a few life changes since I've seen you." Cole's bare chest grazed against her breasts and she jumped. She opened her eyes wide. "Or have you?"

Cole paused. "What do you mean?"

He was so close that she found it difficult to think. It was as if her body had been asleep and now energy sparked inside her. Her heart pounded against her chest and her blood pumped hard through her veins. Her skin stung with awareness. Why? Why did she only feel like this around Cole? It wasn't fair.

A sickening thought occurred to her. "How long have you been a stripper?" she asked. "You're very good at it."

"Should I be flattered by your surprise or insulted?" he asked as he rolled his hips.

Angie curled her fingers tight into fists. She wasn't going to touch him. Hold him. Guide his hips. No, she wasn't, no matter how much her hands tingled with need. "I notice you're not really answering the question," she said, all too aware of how her voice cracked. "Were you stripping when we were together?"

Cole jerked back as if he'd been struck. His smile disappeared and his mouth tightened. "Do you really think that?"

"I don't know what to think." She really hoped he didn't have a secret life, but the man had always been private. He kept things to himself and now she wondered if she knew him at all.

"This is not what it looks like," he said as he kneeled down before her.

She tensed up as her heart pounded faster. "It never is."

"I'm not a stripper." He placed his hands on her knees and pulled them apart.

"Really?" Her voice was high and every muscle in her body locked. How could he touch her so intimately and yet so casually? "Because you're faking it very well."

She looked down at him and tried to fight off the memories. How many times had they been like this? How many times had their position been reversed? Cole knew how to touch her, please her with his hands and mouth. She never found that kind of satisfaction anywhere else.

Cole lifted her leg and placed it over his bare shoulder. Angie saw his expression. She recognized the desire and something else. Something bittersweet. She didn't know why he felt that way. He was the one who walked away.

She couldn't fight the pang of misery. Angie yanked her leg away. She held up her hands in defeat. She couldn't do this. Not with Cole. When they were together, the sex they had was romantic. Intimate. It had meant something. She didn't want to respond to the same routine he did for any woman who had a dollar. "This lap dance is over."

"Not yet." Still kneeling between her legs, Cole slowly slid his body up against hers.

Angie inhaled sharply as she remembered every plane and angle of his body. How it felt to curl up against his hard chest, cling to his broad shoulders and wrap her legs against his waist.

She felt the sweat beading on her skin and tried to remain calm. She saw the knowing twinkle in Cole's eyes. Did he remember, too? Or did he know the effect he had on her? Angie looked away. "I'm not sure what you're trying to accomplish here...."

"Then this must be your first time at a strip club."

She turned back and frowned at him. "But you're wasting your time with me."

Cole gave a crooked smile. "It's never a waste of time being with you."

She stilled as the words washed over her. How could he say that when he'd dumped her and never stayed in touch? "We're done."

"No, wait." He quickly straddled her legs and grabbed the back of her chair again. She was trapped and considered pushing him away. But that meant touching him. Pressing her hands against his naked skin... "I have something to tell you."

"Yeah, I got it." She searched for a safe spot to focus

on, trying not to notice the way his broad chest rose and fell, or how his rock-hard abs gleamed with sweat from dancing. "I heard what you said. You're not really a stripper. Let me guess. You're in between jobs. You're doing a favor for a friend?"

He thrust his hips to the music. "I'm undercover."

Angie slowly shifted her gaze to meet his. That was one excuse she didn't expect. A chuckle erupted from her throat. "That's a good one."

Cole stopped moving and frowned. "You're not supposed to laugh while getting a lap dance."

"I'm sorry. I can't help it." She shook her head as she continued to laugh. "It's not like I'm pointing."

He sighed and moved forward until his mouth was against her ear. "Angie, this is serious."

The bubble of laughter died in her throat as she felt his lips against her skin. "Then stop joking." She squirmed away. "I know you're not undercover. You quit the police force after you broke up with me a year ago."

"Hey, Angie, it's my turn," Heidi called out as she approached them.

Angie was unprepared for the fierce territorial streak that sliced through her. She knew Cole was no longer hers, but she couldn't share him. It was bad enough seeing him dance with Brittany. She didn't want him anywhere near Heidi.

"Stall her," Cole demanded.

Angie felt a flash of relief at his reluctance to leave, but she knew it wasn't because he favored her over the others. He needed something from her and it wasn't to relive the memories or have one night together.

"Come on. No playing favorites," Heidi said as she waved a fistful of cash. "I have money to burn."

"Why should I do what you ask?" Angie asked Cole between her teeth. "I should throw you to the wolves."

He looked into her eyes. "I really need to talk to you."

His voice was harsh, but she saw the pleading in his gaze. What was so important? Curiosity got the better of her. She sighed and looked at the maid of honor. "Sorry, Heidi. I'm still waiting for him to rock my world. I'll send him over to you once that happens."

Heidi rolled her eyes. "I'll be back." She stormed off into the crowd of women, who were encouraging the other strippers to take it all off.

"Really?" Cole said. "Like you couldn't come up with something more flattering?"

She shrugged. "I didn't want to set her expectations too high."

Cole did a sinuous roll of his hips that made Angie squeeze her legs together. "Get some money out so you can hold me here longer," he suggested.

Angie shook her head. "I told you that I don't have any cash."

"You always have money in case of emergencies."

She was surprised that he would remember that. For some reason she assumed he'd forgotten all about her when he'd moved on. "This is not an emergency."

"Angie," he warned.

She pressed her lips together as she considered her options. She decided to do as he asked if it meant she didn't have to share him with the others. "Fine." She reached inside the front pocket of her skinny jeans and pulled out a twenty. "What will this get me?"

He shook his head and clucked his tongue with regret. "You're not ready for that."

"Don't be too sure," she said with an angry smile.

She wasn't going to let him see how his assumption hurt. "Now what do you need to tell me?"

COLE HESITATED. SHOULD he tell Angie? He hadn't planned on it. Was he considering it just to prove he wasn't a stripper? No, he decided. He needed her help and her insight. In the past he had no problems confiding to her about his job when he worked in Missing Persons. He trusted her and valued her advice.

And his instincts told him that he could still trust her. She wouldn't do anything to hurt him or sabotage his assignment. He didn't have a lot of faith in people, but Angie was different. She would help him even though they were no longer a couple.

Angie moved to get up. "It was good seeing you, Cole, but I was about to call a cab and leave."

"You can't leave," he said, refusing to move out of the way. His hands clenched the back of her chair. He didn't want her to go. It had been too long since he'd seen her and it was difficult to keep up the pretense while he was conducting surveillance. There were a few times when he wanted to forget about his professional distance and approach Angie. Now she was right next to him and he wanted the moment to last.

"Why?" she asked as she crossed her arms. "No one will notice."

He would, but she wouldn't care about that. "The bride will. She'll never forgive you."

"How would you—" Her voice faded when he abruptly turned around. He grabbed her hands and rubbed them against his chest and he swayed to the music. "What are you doing?"

"Keeping my cover," he said. He dragged her hand down his chest until her fingers brushed against his waistband. His stomach clenched as she lowered her hand even more before she snatched it away.

"Will you stop that?" She pushed against his back. "It's kind of hard to listen when you're distracting me with those moves."

He paused and turned to face her. "I'm a private investigator."

She nodded. "You went over to the dark side?"

"Yeah, I did." He liked being a cop, but this was something he needed to do. His goal was to find missing relatives and reunite families. He always wanted to do that ever since he was a teenager.

Angie narrowed her eyes as she watched his face carefully. "Let me see your P.I. license."

He clenched his jaw. This was a side of Angie he hadn't experienced before. He didn't like how she questioned his word. "It's not like I have it on me."

"You don't have to make up a story for me. So you're a stripper and you take your clothes off for a living. I'm not going to judge." She tilted her head and pursed her lips. "Much."

"Why don't you believe me?" he asked irritably.

"I don't know." She shrugged. "But I'm very curious what you would do for a twenty. Is it something I've seen before?"

Cole stopped moving and slowly stood to his full height as the cold anger seeped through him. "Are you comparing what we had together with this?"

"Don't worry." Angie held up a hand as if it would erase his hurt and frustration. "I get the feeling that there is no comparison. You needed to find excitement elsewhere and this is where you wound up. How could I possibly have competed with this?" She splayed her hands out and gestured at the club.

"I didn't leave you for this," he said through clenched teeth. The anger gripped his chest and he took a deep breath. "I really am a private investigator."

"Mmm-hmm. And you needed to infiltrate a strip club? Why? Are the guys jewel thieves by day?" She made a show of looking around her before she leaned forward and stage-whispered, "Is Tiger really an assassin?"

"I'm investigating the maid of honor."

"Say what?" Her voice went high. "Heidi?"

Cole clapped his hand over her mouth before she said any more. "Yes. And don't look for her. We can't let Heidi know we're talking about her."

"Heidi," she repeated against his hand. She pulled his hand away. "Why are you investigating her?"

"I can't tell you. I've already said too much." He had to keep some things confidential but he wanted Angie to know what he was doing with his life. Despite the fact they were no longer together, he wanted her to be proud of his accomplishments.

She pressed her fingers against her forehead as if she were trying to wrap her mind around the news. "Heidi is not interesting enough to have a secret life."

"Don't blow this for me." He looked over his shoulder. Everyone was still cheering as Tiger and Robin played up to their audience. He didn't see Heidi in the crowd.

"You already blew your best bet for the night. Heidi wanted a lap dance from you. Why are you wasting your time with me?"

He refused to give a lap dance to Heidi or any other woman in this club. It was different with Angie. "I can't interrogate her while I'm thrusting in her face."

"That would require special coordination," Angie admitted. "But listen, I won't say anything to Heidi."

"Thank you." He stood between Angie's legs but was reluctant to leave. "One more thing."

"Oh, my God, what?" She looked upward and groaned with frustration. "I swear this is the longest lap dance in history."

"What can you tell me about Heidi?" he asked. "What do your instincts tell you?"

Angie's eyes widened as if she were shocked. "Is this why you came over?" she asked indignantly. "To pump me for information?"

"It's not the *only* reason." He also had to stop her from telling anyone about his work history. But he wasn't about to mention that to Angie.

"I don't know much about her," Angie said through clenched teeth, "But I can tell you that she's no criminal mastermind."

"What's your impression?" He could rely on her opinion. Angie had to figure people out very quickly as a personal trainer.

"She's shallow. Fake," Angie stated. "Doesn't play well with others."

From the surveillance he'd done, that could describe the bride and the other bridesmaid. "What else?"

"She's very loyal to Britt— Hey—" she flattened her hand against her chest "—I'm not your informant. If you want to know anything, go give a lap dance to Brittany's assistant. Cheryl knows everyone and everything about this wedding."

Cole sighed. There were occasions when he really questioned what he had to do for his job. *Think of the end result. You are bringing a family back together.*

You are giving someone else the happy ending you didn't get.

"Here." She thrust her twenty-dollar bill in front of him. "Don't let me keep you."

Cole looked at the money and waited. He had called in a lot of favors to masquerade as a stripper for his surveillance, but it had been made very clear that he had to act like the other dancers. No exceptions. "I can't take it like that. House rules."

She made a face. "Like there's a policy?"

"Actually, there is." He smiled, knowing Angie wasn't going to like what he had to say. "If you don't want to put it in my pants, I can take it with my teeth. But first you would have to put it between your—"

"All right! I'll just give it to you."

Cole braced his legs and laced his hands behind his head. He leaned back and tilted his hips forward. He watched Angie silently, wondering what her next move would be. He assumed she would be quick, but instead Angie curled her fingers around the waistband of his leather pants.

His muscles clenched as her knuckles rubbed against his hipbone. Cole hissed in a breath as he felt his penis get hard. He wasn't going to be able to hide his reaction. It would take the last of his self-control not to take her hand and press it against his erection.

Cole closed his eyes, praying for restraint, when a frightened scream ripped through the air. He whirled around and instinctively held Angie back when she jumped from her chair.

"Over there." Angie motioned at Brittany, who stood by an empty table. The bride-to-be pointed at the floor.

Cole ran forward. He felt Angie right behind him.

There was something about that scream that had sent a chill down his spine.

He saw a woman lying on the floor, partially under a table. She was facedown and a tablecloth hid her from the waist up. All he saw were two legs and silver stilettos.

"It's Heidi," Angie said.

3

"BACK UP," ANGIE ordered the women surrounding Heidi. She followed Cole, pushing her way through the crowd. "Give her some space."

Angie crouched down next to Heidi and watched Cole carefully roll her onto her back. She knew first aid and CPR for her job, but she was glad he was with her. He was calm and in control during times of crisis. She knew she could depend on him.

"Someone call an ambulance," she called out to the crowd as Cole checked the maid of honor's airway.

"I'm on it," Cheryl said as she got her phone out of her tiny purse.

"What do we have here?" she asked Cole. She slid Heidi's golden bracelet aside so she could check the woman's pulse. She noticed Heidi's skin was warm to the touch.

"Airways are clear and she's breathing." The relief in his voice was unmistakable.

"Pulse is strong." Angie addressed the other guests. "What happened? Did anyone see her fall? Did she faint?"

She saw the women shrug and shake their heads. From the murmurs and snatches of conversation, it was clear that no one had seen Heidi after her lap dance. She had her spotlight and then melted back into the crowd.

"Is she on anything?" Cole asked in a low, confidential tone.

"I have no idea." She had spent a lot of time with Heidi in the past week, but she wasn't that knowledgeable about the maid of honor.

"I didn't catch that." Brittany was at Cole's side. Her movements were choppy and frantic. "What did you ask?"

"Is she on any medication?" Angie quickly rephrased the question and Cole gave her a look of gratitude.

"How should I know?" Brittany tossed up her hands as her voice rose to a shriek. "Check her purse."

Angie looked around. The floor was sticky and pink from a spilled drink and a martini glass was next to Heidi's hand. She found the handbag under the table and opened it. "Cell phone. Credit card. Dollar bills. Lipstick."

Cole glanced up. "That's it?"

Angie had thought the same thing. For someone who was as high-maintenance as Heidi, she expected more. At least a bag of beauty products. "I don't think anything is missing. This purse is too small."

"Keys? Driver's license?"

"I don't think she brought them along," Angie said. "She took the party bus like the rest of us."

"We should roll her onto her side."

Angie knew why Cole suggested that. Heidi could vomit if she was intoxicated or under the influence.

They eased her sideways and put her in the recovery position.

To her, it was very obvious how she and Cole still worked in sync. In the past they could share a mere look and understand. Or she could say a word—not a sentence, not even a phrase—and Cole would know what she was talking about. She thought the year apart would diminish their shorthand communication, but it was all still there.

"Does anyone have a jacket I can use?" Angie asked the other women. "Something to keep her warm while we wait for the ambulance?"

"I'll go find something," Cheryl said before she hurried away.

Cole gently tipped Heidi's head back to keep the airways open. He went still when he cupped her head. Angie was immediately aware of his wariness. That was one thing she wished had disappeared since they broke up. She was too aware of him. She knew the instant when his mood shifted. He would show no change in expression but somehow she knew.

She leaned over Heidi and blocked Cole's face from the crowd. "What is it?" she asked.

He pulled his hand away. She saw the dark stain on his fingers. "Blood."

"What did she fall on?" She examined the table next to Heidi. There was no blood on the white tablecloth.

Cole's expression was grim. He leaned forward to whisper in her ear. "I think she got hit."

"With what?" She glanced around. All the tables and chairs were in place. The metallic vases were upright and not a flower was out of place. The drinking glasses were plastic. She had no idea what could be used as a weapon.

"This isn't happening," Brittany wailed as she stomped off. "I should have known Heidi would do this to me."

Robin ran over to her and wrapped her arms around Brittany's shoulders. "It's going to be okay."

"How can you say that?" Brittany started to cry. "My party is ruined."

Angie rolled her eyes and moved closer to recheck Heidi's pulse. "Remind me never to be around Brittany when there's an emergency."

"I recommend staying clear when she finds out one of her friends did this."

COLE SQUINTED AS he checked out the strip club. The building was a lot different when all the lights were on and the music stopped. The paramedics had left with Heidi on a stretcher and now the place felt barren and deserted. The white tablecloths and colorful flower arrangements couldn't hide the utilitarian setting.

"Anything else?" he asked Linda, the first officer on the scene. He remembered her from the force. Sometimes he missed the camaraderie at the police station. He missed having a partner. Having backup.

"Yeah, I really like the outfit, Foster," Linda said as she tapped her pen against her notebook. "It's so you."

He crossed his arms and glared at her. He couldn't wait to get out of these leather pants and put a shirt on. "Yeah, yeah, yeah. I've already heard it from the other guys. I'm sure all the customers are curious about how I know everyone."

"They can think you're friends with a few guys in law enforcement. Get over it. We have more important concerns. Now let me go over this statement again."

Cole took a deep breath. Linda was right. It didn't

matter if they found out he was an ex-cop or a private investigator. He needed to know what happened to Heidi. It bothered him that he got distracted and she was injured on his watch.

"So," Linda began as she perused her notes, "you were giving a lap dance."

He pressed his lips together. "I was undercover."

She raised her eyebrows. "To your ex-girlfriend."

"She's a bridesmaid." He glanced over to Angie. She was sitting alone, her arms and legs crossed, her face tilted away from the rest of the guests. She was quiet and thoughtful while the others chatted or used their cell phones.

"And the lap dance was how long?"

"I wasn't keeping track." Cole spotted Linda holding back a smile. He winced. He was never going to hear the end of this. "What hospital is the victim going to? I should notify her family."

The woman's smile disappeared and she gave a nod, sliding back into her professional demeanor. "I'll find out and get back to you."

"Thanks." He gestured back to where they had found Heidi on the floor. "What do you think happened?"

Linda shrugged. "I think drinking and high heels don't mix."

He shook his head. "I don't think that's it. Something is not right."

"You suspect foul play? Because I don't see that. I see it as bad luck. Is there something about your case that you're not sharing?"

"It's about the angle that she fell. We found her face-first but her injury was on the back of her head. And why didn't she break her fall with her hands?"

"That doesn't necessarily mean someone hurt her." Linda pocketed her notepad and stepped away. "We'll find out more when she regains consciousness."

Cole rubbed his hands over his face. He had found Heidi two weeks ago and had been investigating her life. He wished he had more answers.

He turned and walked over to Angie. He paused in midstep. Was that wise? She was distracting him. It would be best to talk to the other women and to ignore her presence.

No, he couldn't do that. He quietly sat down next to Angie. He wasn't sure what to say but he wanted to be there for her. He knew what she was like after a scare or an emergency. She did what needed to be done and then her adrenaline kicked in. He wanted to keep watch over her.

"Why are you sitting all the way over here?" he asked. Angie was always friendly and could talk to anyone about anything. He always liked that about her and wished he could be the same. It was a skill he had to develop for his job but it didn't come easy.

"I'm about ready to tackle Brittany if she doesn't shut up," she answered. "I'd rather not do it in front of the police."

Yes, he'd made the right decision. He would have to watch her closely or she would let her emotions get the best of her.

"Don't you find it weird that Brittany hasn't shown any concern for Heidi?" Cole asked as he watched the bride-to-be pace the floor. "All she's worried about is whether this affects her wedding ceremony."

"You never know how someone will react in a stressful situation," Angie said. She paused and glanced at him. "But, honestly, I expected this from Brittany."

"Why?" Brittany wailed as she sat down with a thump. Several women rushed over to pull her back up. "Why did she have to have an accident right before the wedding?"

"Does she expect you to go over there?" Cole asked. "You are a bridesmaid. Isn't taking care of her one of your duties?"

"Not going to happen," Angie said. "What did the police say about Heidi? Was it an accident?"

"The police are treating it as one. I can't say that it wasn't." He hoped it was an accident. If someone harmed her, he had no evidence of motive or means.

"I warned her not to wear those heels!" Brittany's voice rang through the club.

"Great, now she's revising history." Angie slid down in her chair. "You may have to hold me back."

He knew it was all talk. Angie could take down a man twice her size but the only time he'd seen her use those skills was in the bedroom. Cole smiled as he remembered those lighthearted moments and the hot sex that came after. He shifted restlessly in his seat and tried to focus on something else. "How do you know she's not telling the truth?"

"Brittany told Heidi to buy those shoes," Angie said. "We were at the mall picking up last-minute stuff for the party."

Cole watched the police leave the scene. "Seems like everyone can go home now. I can finally get out of these leather pants."

"And this bachelorette party from hell has officially ended." She tensed beside him. "Brittany is coming over here. I will not be held accountable for my actions."

"Think of Patrick," he advised. "The guy has been your best friend for years."

"That should count for something. He's only known Brittany for a year."

"Doesn't matter," he said, feeling suddenly weary. He knew from experience that Angie needed to take a step back and keep her mouth shut or she would regret it. "Patrick will choose Brittany's side over yours every time. Take my word for it."

Angie gave him a sharp look as if his advice revealed something she hadn't seen in him. He was almost grateful that Brittany was suddenly standing in front of Angie.

"We'll need an emergency meeting," Brittany told Angie as she tried to wipe the mascara streaks with a tissue. "Meet up at the usual Starbucks tomorrow afternoon at four."

"Why?" Angie asked. "Are we going to visit Heidi?"

"We don't have time for that," Brittany said, dismissing the suggestion with the wave of her hand. "We have to decide what happens if Heidi can't be maid of honor. A groomsman will need to be let go. Then we have to rework the processional and recessional. I really don't need this extra work."

"Your maid of honor was seriously injured at the bachelorette party," Angie reminded her.

"Careful," Cole muttered.

"Shouldn't you postpone the wedding? Maybe downsize it?" she said hopefully.

Brittany took a step closer. "I'm already down one bridesmaid."

Angie frowned and her mouth was set in a straight line. "But…"

"Angie—" Brittany's voice dropped "—I have

planned my wedding for years. I have waited for this day. Nothing and no one is going to get in my way."

Cole didn't like the threat he heard in Brittany's voice. He grasped Angie's forearm, reminding her that he was there as backup. He was tempted to pull her behind him and wedge himself between Angie and Brittany.

Angie went rigid. He sensed her struggle, but after a tense moment, Angie nodded and smiled. "Got it."

"Good." Brittany glared at Angie before she swiveled on her impractical heels and stalked off. "Be at Starbucks by four."

Cole watched the bride-to-be leave. Every step pulsed with hostility. "What would happen if you didn't show?" he asked Angie. "Would you get kicked out of the bridal party?"

"Oh, if only," she said as she pulled from his grasp.

Cole studied Angie. "You're really not enjoying this wedding."

"I have to deal with that," she said, gesturing at Brittany, "and I have spent way too much money on the dress. Brittany also expects us to attend all these events. I've been to six wedding showers. Six! I don't think I can take much more."

"You can't miss anything?" An idea started to form.

"Not one! Which is why I had to take off work for the next week." She stopped and took a long, deep breath then released it. "I shouldn't complain. This is Patrick's wedding and I'm glad he wants me to be part of it."

"But?" he asked as they walked to the exit.

"This wedding is a train wreck and nothing is going to stop it."

"Do you want it to stop?" Was she worried about her

friend? Did she feel the need to take matters into her own hands? No, he discarded that idea immediately. That was not Angie's idea of friendship.

"I would never sabotage a wedding— Wait." She whirled around and looked at him. Her eyes narrowed as she considered the meaning behind his question. "Do you think I tried?"

"No." He'd always admired Angie's loyalty to her friends and family. She tried to be supportive even if she didn't understand their choices.

"Because there has been one setback after the next now that I think about it. So many…but I've been helping to fix the problems. Patrick wants Brittany to have the perfect wedding and I'm doing everything I can."

Cole raised his hands in surrender. "I believe you."

She pointed her finger at him. "And if you think I had something to do with Heidi's accident—"

"Whoa! It never crossed my mind. I'm your alibi, remember?"

Angie poked at his chest. "I want to get this wedding over and done with. That's all."

"That's not surprising since you have to go to every event." He needed that kind of access if he was going to find out more about Heidi and her accident.

"Weddings used to be so simple," Angie said as she continued walking. "When I get married, it's going to be on a beach with a few friends and a minister. Shoes optional."

Cole felt the weight of regret settle in his chest when he heard those words. *When* she got married. Did she have someone in mind or was this in theory? All he knew was that he wasn't part of those plans.

Angie dipped her head as if she were embarrassed for mentioning her ideal wedding to an ex. "I should get going," she said, awkwardly motioning at the door. "I hope your undercover work goes well."

"Thanks," he said gruffly. "You need a ride?"

"No, I'm on the party bus," she said as she moved backward. Her steps were slow, as if she wanted to say something more.

"Angie?" Cole hesitated. He wasn't sure if he should do this. If he should say anything. If he had any other option, he wouldn't pursue this.

She kept walking backward. "Yeah?"

He shifted from one foot to the other. This was probably a bad idea. "I know we didn't end well and I'm really sorry about that, but…"

She stopped walking. "Yeah?"

"I need to get into the wedding." He said the words in a rush. "Are you going with anyone?"

4

"The nerve of that man," Angie muttered to herself. "Did he think I would jump at the chance to take him?" He most likely did. She had never denied him anything in the past.

Angie blew out a puff of air as she ran around the empty high school track. It was a cold and damp morning. The evergreen trees, spindly and clustered together, did nothing to stop the breeze as the sun weakly shone through the haze of clouds. She splashed through the puddles from last night's rain and kept moving.

Most people would be reluctant to get out of bed on this kind of day. She had wanted to toss the covers over her head and act like last night didn't happen. Push away the memory of Heidi injured and unconscious. Forget about Brittany and her demands. Erase Cole completely out of her mind.

Seeing Cole Foster last night had left her unsettled. Every time she tried to sleep, her fragmented dreams were about him, bare-chested and wearing leather pants. Only this time, she boldly touched his muscular body. In her dreams, she encouraged him for more. She wasn't afraid to take charge.

Angie clenched her teeth and pumped her arms and legs harder. What was it about that man? When she had been with him, she'd felt like she could ask for anything. Try everything. But she had gone too far. Deep down, she must have known. She had held back from exploring her fantasies until she felt secure in the relationship. But it didn't matter how long she waited. He still ran.

She thought he was different from the other guys. She heard enough boasting to know the men in her world liked their women clingy and submissive. She couldn't be like that. She was forthright and a little impatient, but she was never aggressive in bed until she was with Cole. She didn't ask for anything she wouldn't give to him.

But apparently he didn't like a strong and powerful woman in bed. A woman who made it very clear how much she wanted him and what she wanted from him. She had felt safe but excited. She trusted he wouldn't judge her, wouldn't think less of her. When she had looked into his eyes, she felt like a goddess. But she had been wrong. She had mistaken adoration with intimidation. She had scared him off.

She had learned her lesson. Next time, she would allow the man to take the lead. From now on she would keep her fantasies to herself.

If she wanted to feel strong and powerful, she'd focus on other parts of her life. Like her job and on the track. There she would be encouraged to push herself to the limits. There she could shine.

Angie rounded the bend and saw someone standing at the gate that led to the parking lot. Her steps faltered when she recognized the car parked next to hers. Her heart kicked against her ribs when she saw that it was Cole waiting for her.

Why was this happening? Angie's chest tightened at the sight of him. She hadn't seen him for a year and thought he had moved out of Seattle. They had never crossed paths since he returned. Now she'd seen him twice in two days. She wasn't sure if she was ready to deal with him again. How often would she look at him and think of the broken dreams and the ruined promise of a future together?

And it wasn't fair, she decided as she maintained her pace. Cole still had the ability to make her pulse skip hard. While she was expected to put effort in her appearance, Cole could throw on some clothes and still manage to look sexy.

Her gaze traveled down the length of his body. The blue buttoned-down shirt skimmed his lean, muscular chest and strong arms. He had incredible strength but he could still gently embrace her. Her gaze lowered and she noticed his faded jeans that emphasized his powerful legs. She always admired how he moved with lethal grace, yet she could outrun him.

She had always been attracted to his mix of force and restraint. He liked to dress casually but had a commanding presence. He spoke with authority in his low, husky voice. Her heart would do a slow flip whenever she saw a twinkle in his dark blue eyes or a curve of a smile on his stern mouth.

As she got closer, she saw his serious expression. The lines on his tired face were deep. It looked as if he hadn't slept.

No, she wasn't going to feel sorry. It wasn't her job to worry or look after him. She wasn't his girlfriend anymore. She didn't want to see him. Feel anything for him. She felt too raw, too unprepared.

But she couldn't avoid him. She had a few more laps to go, but she knew she wouldn't be able to concentrate with him watching her. If she ignored him here, he would keep at it until she listened. She used to like his persistence. Now, it was just annoying. She knew it was better to get this over and done with.

Angie slowed down and walked to the gate. Her legs were burning and shaking. Sweat glistened on her skin and dampened her gray tank top. Her hair was coming out of the ponytail and she brushed off a few tendrils from her flushed face.

She felt his gaze on her. Her top and shorts felt too small. Her skin tingled and she suddenly didn't know what to do with her hands. She wanted to cross her arms and hide her small breasts. She felt exposed.

She wasn't sure why she felt this way. Cole no longer cared. Heck, at one time she thought he found her sexy. That only showed how delusional she truly was.

Resisting the urge to pull on a jacket or sweatpants, Angie grabbed onto the chain-link fence and started her cooling-down routine. "You're up early."

"I haven't gone to bed," he said quietly as he watched her stretch her legs. "I've been at the hospital."

"I see." She bent down and hesitated when she felt Cole's gaze linger on her legs. "How is Heidi?"

"I'm told she's awake," he said gruffly. "I can't get much information because I'm not a friend or next of kin."

Angie grabbed her foot with one hand and slowly raised her leg behind her. She immediately realized her mistake. She wanted to stretch her quadriceps, but it required her to thrust her chest out. Her nipples tightened and her breasts felt full and heavy. She glanced at Cole just as he dragged his gaze from her breasts to her face. She abruptly looked away.

"Why are you here?" she asked as she dropped her leg. She could skip her cooling-down routine for today. "You're not dressed for a run."

"I need your help." He reached out and offered her the water bottle she had placed next to the gate. "Heidi's family in California hired me to track her down. I've done that and I informed my clients about what happened."

"What does that have to do with me?" she asked. She grabbed the water bottle, careful not to graze her fingers against his.

"I have to find out what caused the accident. She had a wild lifestyle a while back. Her family wants to know if she's still into that. If they need to get her some help."

"I don't know anything about Heidi," she reminded him as she took a sip. Her throat didn't seem to want to cooperate as Cole watched her drink. She wiped the water away from her mouth with the back of her hand. "I don't think I can help."

"You have access," he pointed out.

She glared at him. "Is this about you going to the wedding? I already said no." She didn't even have to think about it. The word had fallen from her lips. She had been stunned by his request. How could he ask her on a date—even a fake one—when he had broken her heart? Didn't he have any feelings?

"I need more than a wedding invite," he explained. "I need total access. The rehearsal dinner. Behind the scenes."

"It's not necessary." Angie shook her head and

started for her car. "Heidi may be out of the wedding, period. She has a head injury."

"But the people at the bachelorette party would be there," he said softly.

She stopped and turned. "You don't think it was an accident."

"It could be an accident. The police think so, and I haven't seen any information about her blood alcohol level," he admitted. "I think someone may have tried to hurt Heidi. It probably had something to do with her private life. I just don't know how they did it."

"Private life?" She thought that was an odd choice of words and she thought about the other comments he'd made about Heidi. She lifted her chin when she realized what he was trying not to say. "You mean drugs. That's why you asked if she was on something."

His eyes widened with admiration. "Good catch. I don't know if she's still using."

She pursed her lips as she tried to remember how Heidi had acted over the past few days. "I haven't seen any signs of it."

"You weren't looking for signs, but maybe if I hung around while you were preparing for the wedding…" he said hopefully as he let his words trail off.

Angie sighed and crossed her arms. "Why do you have to drag me into this?"

"Why won't you let me be your date?" he countered.

"I think it's obvious." It didn't matter if it was a pretend date. Spending a day with Cole would remind her of what she once had with him. What she had lost.

Cole's jaw tightened. "Are you taking someone else?"

She went still. Angie would love to lie and avoid any

discussion on her nonexistent love life. But it wouldn't take much for him to find out the truth. "No."

His blue eyes darkened. "Will someone get jealous if you take me?" he asked stiffly.

She wanted to scoff at the suggestion. "No."

He spread his arms out. "Then what's the problem?"

He didn't get it. How was that possible? For a private detective, Cole Foster was oblivious. "I don't have to give you a reason." She turned and marched to her car.

"Come on, Angie," he said right behind her.

"After all," she said, "you didn't give me a reason why you broke up with me."

"Is that what this is all about?" His voice rose with incredulity. "I told you why I needed to break up with you."

"You weren't ready for a relationship." She yanked her car door open. "It's you, not me." She threw the water bottle into the backseat with more force than necessary. "Something about how I deserved better."

"You do," he said quietly.

She wasn't going to fall for the sincerity in his voice. No, what Cole really meant was that *he* deserved better. "Are you dating anyone?" she asked huskily as the emotions clawed her throat. "Wouldn't she be upset if you started hanging around your ex? Or would she understand that it was just for an assignment?"

"There hasn't been anyone since you."

Angie didn't realize how much she needed to hear those words until he had spoken them. If he'd been in a relationship with someone else, it would have destroyed her. "I find that hard to believe," she said hoarsely.

"It's true." He took a step closer. She took a step back and bumped up against her car. "I've spent all my time and energy building up my agency."

"And what's up with that?" she asked, her voice rising. "Not once did you talk to me about having your own business. You were passionate about what you did. About working with Missing Persons."

"It's still what I do," he said, his eyes sparking with annoyance. It was clear he didn't want to discuss it. "My agency specializes in tracing people. Reuniting families."

"I thought everything was fine and then it was like you changed overnight." And it wasn't easy to ignore when his abrupt change occurred. It was right after she lowered her guard. Once she started taking charge in the bedroom.

Her face burned as she remembered that. She had felt sexy and desirable. Strong and assertive. She thought Cole loved it. That he wanted her to reveal this side she didn't share with anyone else. Those moments had been special. Intimate.

She had only been fooling herself. Seeing what she wanted to see. She thought they were solid as a couple, but she was blindsided when he dumped her two weeks later. He had walked away, saying he couldn't give her what she needed.

But what he really meant was that she was undesirable. Unwanted. Her fantasies were not his. She couldn't give him what he needed. She had given him everything but she hadn't been good enough.

"I didn't mean to hurt you." His whisper was heavy with regret.

She straightened up and offered a tight smile. "I'm over it," she lied. "I just thought you were different from the other guys."

Cole frowned. "What do you mean by that?"

"That you weren't in it for the challenge." What a

few men had tried to do in the past. To take on Angie Lawson. Soften her up and tame the tomboy.

COLE TOOK A step back and stared at Angie. "You think I dated you because I like a challenge?"

Angie was a challenge, all right. She was stubborn and impatient. Independent almost to a fault. She was brazen but he also saw the insecurities she tried to hide.

"I don't know why and I don't care," she declared. "All I know is that I'm not going to put myself through that again."

"Angie, our time together meant a lot to me. I can't tell you how difficult it was to leave you." It had been the hardest thing for him to do, but it had been necessary. He had started to think he could be with Angie forever. That she could fall in love with him. But that was a fantasy. Even if he tried harder and tried to be better, he wasn't worthy of love. His family had proven that to him years ago.

Cole stepped away from Angie and looked down. He didn't want her to see the struggle in his eyes. "Angie, it's very hard for me to ask, but I need your help."

He felt her hesitation. She was the kind of woman who automatically offered her help, but it was different now. He knew how awkward it was to offer help to someone who had once discarded you.

"You were always there when I needed you." He hated how his voice cracked. Hated how much her loyalty had meant to him. "And I was there for you."

"We were a couple then," she said softly.

"You are still very important to me." She was the most important person in his life, but he couldn't tell her that. Angie wouldn't believe him, anyway.

"So important that you couldn't stay in touch?" she asked bitterly.

He dragged his gaze to meet hers. Staying in touch would have been a constant reminder of what he couldn't have. "I thought a clean break would be best. It hasn't been easy for me, either. It still isn't."

"And you think that being my date for the wedding will make it better?"

"No, but I think we're at a point where we can be friendly with each other. Do you really want to deal with that bride on your own? Think of me as backup."

"She is unbearable," she said as she considered his suggestion. "It would be nice to show up with a stripper boyfriend."

He jerked back. "Say what?"

"Most of the wedding guests will think that you're a stripper." Angie bit her lip as she tried to contain her smile. "Patrick and some of the other guys will know the truth but I could tell them that our breakup sent you into a tailspin."

He had crashed and burned once he left Angie. It had taken him nearly a year to get back on his feet. "You want me to continue the role as a stripper?"

"Why not? You're the one who started it. And no one would question my sudden wedding date. After all, you showed me special attention last night. Thanks for that."

He ignored her sarcasm. "You're really considering this?"

"Brittany is going to have a fit that I'm bringing a date at such late notice." She grimaced as if she were imagining the bride's reaction. "I'll talk to Cheryl, her assistant. She's in charge of the details."

"Think you can get me into Heidi's room today?"

He knew he was already pushing her, but he was running against the clock. If he didn't get answers in the next few days, chances were he never would.

"I was going to visit her today after Brittany's meeting," she revealed reluctantly. "I'll meet you at the hospital and we'll go in together."

"Thank you," he said. He wasn't sure if the relief he felt was because he could move forward with his assignment or because Angie was on his side once more.

Angie gave a sharp nod and got into her car. "By the way, my stripper boyfriend is totally into me," she said. "He can't believe his luck that he landed me."

"I can do that." He wouldn't even have to pretend. He had felt that way since she had accepted his invitation for a first date. He had no idea what he did to convince her and often felt he was living on borrowed time. He knew someday she would wake up and see she could do much better than him.

"But I'm not really into him," Angie warned Cole. "Everyone would get suspicious if I was all clingy and affectionate."

Especially since she didn't act that way in public, Cole thought. But when they had been alone, she was very demonstrative and explicit in her requests. "So it's only physical attraction?" he teased.

She grinned. "Yeah, something like that."

"Then that will be our cover. By the end of today, everyone will think we're having a red-hot but brief reunion," he promised. It had to be short-term for his sanity. One touch from her and he'd want another. One kiss and he wouldn't stop. Unless this had a predetermined end date, he'd start to believe he had another chance. He'd forget that she never loved him—couldn't love him—in the first place.

"A wild fling?" Her smile disappeared. "No one will believe that."

"They will." Because he was going to make the most of this temporary affair. "I guarantee it."

5

"THIS WAS A bad idea." Angie felt her ponytail swing against her shoulders as she strode down the hospital corridor. She was nervous and it showed. She took a deep breath and gripped the flower arrangement tighter.

"Don't back out on me now." Cole draped his arm around her shoulder.

A sense of longing crashed through her unexpectedly and she tried not to react. It had been common for Cole to touch or hold her whenever they were together. She shouldn't be so surprised.

"Oh, are we pretending to be a couple already?" she asked lightly as she struggled with the opposing needs to shake off his touch and to curl into his body. "Heidi can't see us from here."

"You don't start pretending the minute you walk into the room," he explained. "You assume the role as soon as possible. And you never know whom you're going to bump into on the way. What if we see someone from the bridal party?"

Angie pressed her lips together. Cole always had an

answer for everything, but she didn't think this was going to work. "No one will believe this."

"That we're together?" He stopped and looked down at her, his arm cradling her closer. "No one questioned it when we were dating."

Was he kidding? His friends probably didn't ask or care. She wished she had been so lucky. Her relatives teased her about how opposites attract. Her female clients asked if she used any sexual expertise in grabbing Cole's attention. One acquaintance had asked why Cole was dating her when he could have any woman.

She guessed no one dared to ask Cole those questions. Lucky him. "I mean that no one would think I would hook up with a stripper."

It didn't help that she had done nothing different with her appearance. Angie knew she should have worn something suggestive or pretty. She winced at the thought. Instead she wore her favorite standbys. The white long-sleeve T-shirt and black track pants were comfortable and her running shoes were top-of-the-line.

She should have given her appearance more thought. After all, she was going to stand next to Cole Foster, whose masculine beauty was emphasized in a blue henley shirt and jeans. Most guys in Seattle wore that combination, but for some reason, Cole stood out in the crowd. It wasn't just her opinion. She had seen more than one person in the hall give him a flirtatious glance.

"But it's not unreasonable that you would backslide," he argued. "Ex sex happens more than you think. Why do you think they give it a name?"

Ex sex. She didn't like that label. It made something that was so emotional into something very casual. She imagined most people had sex with their ex because it would offer some familiarity and comfort. She never had that with Cole. When they were together it had been an exciting roller-coaster ride.

Sometimes the intimacy they had shared felt risky. There were moments that had changed her and made her see Cole differently. Those were the times when she felt they had formed a stronger bond. Backsliding wouldn't let her recapture those life-transforming experiences.

She stumbled to a stop and pretended that she was reading the room numbers. Why was she thinking about that? They weren't backsliding. Cole had no interest in having sex with her. If she responded to any of his gestures or touches, then she would be in trouble. She felt jittery and alive next to him. She was very aware of his clean, masculine scent, how warm and large his hand felt against her shoulder.

"Okay, Heidi's room is over there." She pointed at the door across the hall. "Ready?"

"Yes." He squeezed her arm and drew her closer. "Just follow my lead."

"Wait a second. Let me do the talking," she suggested. "It would look weird if you started asking questions."

Cole showed no expression but she felt the tension in his body. Did he think she would mess up? Or was it hard for him to give up any control in his case? He obviously didn't like it if she took charge in or out of bed.

He nodded. "Fine."

"Really?" She wasn't expecting him to yield. But then, he had surrendered quickly in bed and then she paid for it weeks later. "Are you sure?"

"Yes, absolutely. She'll talk to you because she knows you."

"Okay, let's do this." Angie thrust out her chin and walked out of Cole's embrace. She knew he wanted to enter as a loving couple, but that would distract her. It was bad enough that she already felt the loss of his touch. That bothered her. A year without Cole and she was craving for him more than ever.

Angie knocked on the door and peered inside the room. "Heidi? Do you feel up for visitors?"

Heidi's hands flew to her face. "Oh, I look horrible."

"No, not at all," Angie insisted. It was the truth. The woman's short hair was ruffled and her face was pale, but she was still stunning. The hospital gown did nothing to detract from her fragile beauty.

"Who's that?" Heidi asked as Angie set the bouquet of flowers on the bedside table. "Wait a second, you look familiar."

"This is Cole." She only paused for a second before she hooked her arm around his waist and leaned into his body. It felt as good as she remembered. "He was one of the strippers last night."

"You two got together last night?" Heidi stared at Angie, her mouth hanging open with shock. "You landed a stripper? *You* did?"

Angie cast an I-told-you so look at Cole. He seemed more confused by Heidi's reaction than anything. "Well, last night was crazy," she said as she returned her attention to Heidi. "Don't you remember?"

Heidi pressed her hand against her head. "No. A lot of it is fuzzy."

"I don't remember you drinking that much," she said. She felt awkward and didn't know how Heidi would respond. But if there was one thing Angie knew about being a personal trainer, she always broached difficult topics head-on.

Cole reached up and wrapped his finger around the end of her ponytail. She bit her lip, remembering the bite of pressure when he tugged her hair. He did it to get her attention, either to tease or to warn. She'd almost forgotten how they had silently communicated.

"I don't drink. All those calories, you know?" she said in a rush. "It's either juice or water."

"I suggest that to my clients all the time," Angie murmured. Heidi hadn't been drinking? That threw out the theory that she was too drunk to stand. Or was the maid of honor lying? She couldn't remember what Heidi had been drinking. She hadn't paid any attention.

Angie wasn't sure if she could trust Heidi's answer. Avoiding calories was something she expected from Heidi, but it didn't ring true. Angie also remembered the spilled drink next to Heidi when they had placed her in the recovery position.

Angie jumped a little when she felt Cole's fingertips trail down her spine. "Do you know when you'll get out of here?" she asked in a rush.

"I'm under observation. I'm told it's something they have to do for head injuries." Heidi bit her lip as if she were reluctant to say something. "But the strangest thing happened."

"Oh? What?" Angie's breath caught in her throat as Cole dragged his fingers up and down her back. Did he think it was comforting? She was breathing fast as her entire world centered on the gentle caress of his fingertips.

"My parents called to see if I was okay," Heidi said, her eyes wide as she revealed the news. "I haven't talked to them in years. Not since they kicked me out of the family after I...well, there was a time during college when I was out of control. I thought they didn't want to have anything to do with me. I didn't contact them even after I got my life back on track because I thought they gave up on me. I have no idea how they found out where I was or what happened to me."

"I guess they've always been looking out for you," Cole said quietly. "They just needed a reason to reach out."

As Heidi leaned back on her pillow to consider what he said, Angie looked up at Cole and gave him a warning glare. "Well, Heidi, we should go so you can get some rest. I hope you'll still be at the wedding."

Heidi's mouth trembled. "The doctors don't think that will be possible." Tears welled up in her eyes. "I feel terrible about letting Brittany down. She's never going to forgive me."

"Don't worry about her. She—" Angie forgot what she was about to say as she felt Cole's hand glide against the curve of her hip. She had to get out of here before she bucked against his touch. "This wasn't your fault."

"Thanks," Heidi said as she watched Angie move away from Cole and take a few steps for the door. "And thanks for the flowers."

"You're welcome. Get better soon!" Angie hurried out of the room but she couldn't escape. She didn't have to look back to know that Cole was right behind her.

COLE SAID A quick goodbye to Heidi and then followed Angie. She was moving fast, almost breaking into a run. He was tempted to reach out and grab her ponytail. Wrap it around his hand and hold her still.

He caught up with her several rooms down and blocked her path. "What's the rush?"

She looked over her shoulder as if she were focused on a destination. "I had to get out of there before you blew your cover."

She thought he was blowing their cover? He wasn't the one who had bolted. He would have liked to have asked a few more questions but the opportunity was gone. He had to admit, though, that Angie's questions were helpful. She did well for her first interrogation. "We were very convincing."

Angie rolled her eyes and leaned against the wall. "First you talked about the parents as if you had intimate knowledge of the situation," she whispered fiercely. "And then you went a little overboard with the public displays of affection."

Was that why she abruptly ended the interview? Was his touch unbearable to her now? He wanted to stroke her skin and curl her against his side. He wished she would respond by boldly touching him, publicly acknowledging his claim with a simple gesture or touch. Yet she had to get away from him.

Or was it the opposite? Did she still like it when he held her? Was she holding back because this was supposed to be all pretend? It didn't feel pretend to him. Did she also think it felt too much like the real thing? He tried to tamp down the hope billowing inside him.

"You were never this touchy-feely when we were together," she complained.

"Then you are remembering it wrong." Still, she may have a point. In the past, one touch or one look held the promise of something more. Now that wasn't the case and who knew how many chances he would get to hold her like this? This could be his only opportunity to relive these moments.

Angie smoothed her hand over her hair and tilted her head back. "It's too bad Heidi didn't have a lot of information."

"But she did. She said she wasn't drinking."

"Of course she's going to say that," Angie argued. "She doesn't want Brittany mad at her. The fact is there was a spilled martini next to her."

"It doesn't mean she had any of that in her system." He rested his arm against the wall and looked down at Angie. "I really wish I could get my hands on her blood test."

"Good luck with that," Angie said. "I don't know much about investigations but I know the medical staff will protect Heidi's privacy. No one is going to give it to you."

Cole saw a movement from the corner of his eye. "Here comes the other bridesmaid. Let's sell this relationship once and for all."

She gave him a wary look. "What do you have in mind?"

"Just this." He lowered his head and claimed her mouth with his.

Cole knew he was playing with fire. He only intended to skim her lips. But he found that he couldn't pull away. He needed another kiss and then another. He traced her full, soft lips with the tip of his tongue.

Angie opened her mouth and drew him in. Triumph swept through him. He cupped her jaw with both hands and leaned in. She kissed him as if she couldn't get enough of him. Excitement pulsed through Cole as Angie grabbed his shirt and pulled him closer.

"Hey, you two," Robin said loudly. "Get a room."

Cole wrenched away from Angie. Damn it, he thought as he gulped for air. He forgot. He forgot where they were and why they were kissing. Most of all, he forgot that kissing Angie was like sharing a piece of his soul.

"Oh, it's you from last night." Robin gave a sly smile to Angie and tapped her arm with the box of chocolates she held in her hand. "Good for you. I thought the two of you would hit it off."

"What are you doing here, Robin?" Angie asked as she pushed away from the wall. "I thought you didn't like Heidi."

Cole was suddenly taken aback. He knew from surveillance that Robin and Heidi didn't get along, but he didn't think Angie would say it so bluntly. Yet Robin didn't seem to mind.

"Eh," she said and gave a shrug. "The best way to describe it is that we're frenemies."

This was a person he needed to speak to. Robin knew Heidi from the past and could give him some insight. "The doctor just went in to check on Heidi," Cole lied. "It may be a while. Let's get some coffee while we wait. My treat."

"Lead the way," Robin said.

By the time Cole brought the drinks to their table in the café, he noticed that Robin was relaxed and talkative. He was glad Angie didn't start asking questions right away. It surprised him that Angie knew how to approach Robin. The two women were very different. Robin wore impractical heels, skintight jeans and a fussy pink blouse that looked like an explosion of ruffles on her chest. He preferred Angie's casual look and natural beauty.

When Cole gave Angie her drink, Robin noticed

the complicated order written on the disposable coffee cup. "You guys met last night and he already knows your coffee order?"

Angie's mouth opened and closed. She wasn't sure what to say. Cole knew that they had to stick close to the truth if they wanted this ruse to work. "I dated Angie in the past."

"So he is your ex-boyfriend! That explains why you're hanging around during an obligatory hospital visit." She gave Cole a thorough look. "Most one-night stands would find an excuse to get out of it."

"I wasn't ready for the day to end," Cole said as he rested his arm along the back of Angie's chair. "I had to convince her to bring me along."

"Interesting." She studied Angie with narrowed eyes. "I never thought Angie had that kind of pull."

Cole frowned. Why did these women think he wouldn't be interested in Angie? Were they blind? Angie was the most sensual woman he knew. He could see it in every move, every smile.

"Want something to eat?" Angie suddenly asked, obviously determined to change the subject. "Danish?"

"No thanks." She held her hand up. "Food allergies."

Angie rested her arms on the table and leaned forward. "So what's this about you and Heidi being frenemies? Was it because of her drug use?"

Cole reached up and grabbed the tip of her ponytail. He gave it a sharp tug and hoped she understood his message. There were times when Angie's straightforward attitude was a disadvantage. She couldn't bulldoze her way into delicate discussions.

Cole could see Robin look at Angie with caution. "How do you know about that?"

Angie shrugged. "I've heard the rumors."

Robin sighed and made a face. "Brittany could never keep a secret." She looked around the café before she bent forward and spoke softly. "Yeah, Heidi made my life miserable in college. The lying, the stealing. I thought she had cleaned up, but then she winds up in the hospital after a drunken night. I guess I was wrong."

"Sounds like a lot of drama," Angie said sympathetically. "I can't imagine Brittany putting up with that."

"She wouldn't normally, but Heidi was more a groupie than a friend. Brittany is always on the lookout to add to her entourage."

Angie pursed her lips. "She wanted a minion."

Cole gave another tug on Angie's ponytail. Angie silently responded by pulling her hair over her shoulder so he couldn't reach it. He flexed his fingers and held back.

He wished he could interrupt the conversation. Angie was getting Robin to talk but she was skating on thin ice. It was like watching someone on a tightrope. One wrong word and Robin would stop talking. Or worse, she would notice their interest in Heidi.

When he first took on this case, Heidi's family only wanted to locate her. He had been able to track her down so easily that he wondered if the family had even tried. Once he gave the information to his clients, he soon realized that finding her was only the beginning. What they really wanted from him was to do surveillance. He was supposed to follow Heidi and see if she was still having trouble with drugs and alcohol.

He didn't have a definitive answer and he needed to be sure before he gave his report. What if the family didn't welcome Heidi back because they didn't like the answer? Would they only repair the relationship if Heidi met certain conditions?

He needed to know the truth. A lot was at stake. Unfortunately, the investigation wasn't going as planned. The people who knew Heidi best only seemed to remember how she used to be. They gave no insight into her life today.

"Brittany knew that Heidi would put up with a lot of crap to be friends," Robin explained as she took a sip of her coffee. "I think Heidi wanted to be part of everything."

"That's why she agreed to be maid of honor even though she knew it was going to be an ordeal." Angie tapped her hand on the table. "I wondered why anyone would willingly take on that role. Especially after getting that very demanding email that listed all of Brittany's expectations."

"Oh, I bet Heidi jumped at the offer," Robin said with feeling. "If anyone should be maid of honor, it should have been me. I'm the closest sorority sister to Brittany."

Angie clucked her tongue. "You should have gotten the honor."

Cole winced when he heard Angie's sarcastic emphasis on the word *honor,* but Robin didn't seem to clue in. He was beginning to wonder what had happened in the past year that made Angie bitter about weddings.

"I should have," Robin agreed, "but I don't take orders very well. Heidi will do anything for Brittany and she knows it."

Angie nodded slowly. "I'm sure that's it."

"I should go see Heidi before visiting hours are up. Thanks for the coffee," Robin told Cole before she gave him a speculative look. "Will you be at the wedding?"

"Yes, I insisted."

"Interesting." Robin seemed confused as she cast a look at Angie before returning her attention to him. "Save a dance for me," Robin said before she strode away.

Cole waited until she left the café before he spoke to Angie. "That was a close call," he said, his gaze still on the doorway.

"You mean about Heidi's past?" Angie asked. "It could have gone badly, but Robin assumes Brittany said something. She won't track it back to you."

He hoped that was the case, but he wasn't sure how much Robin gossiped. She could relay everything to whomever would listen, or she might be the kind of person who held back pertinent information until she found the right—and most damaging—moment. "Don't you find it strange that Robin isn't maid of honor?"

"No," Angie said as she sipped her coffee. "Robin may feel she's closest to Brittany, but that doesn't mean Brittany feels the same."

"True." But something didn't quite add up. He felt like he was missing something.

"Is everything okay?" Angie set her cup down and watched him carefully. "What are you thinking about? It doesn't look good."

He shoved his hand through his hair and sighed with frustration. "There's something about last night but I can't remember."

Angie reached out and patted his arm. "You'll get it."

He wanted to cover her hand with his. Keep her there and soak in her encouragement. Angie always made him feel like he could accomplish almost anything if he worked hard for it. "Thanks for meeting me here. I appreciate it."

She awkwardly drew her hand away. "You're welcome," she mumbled as she took a hasty sip of her drink.

"You were very good at getting information out of the bridesmaids," he said and watched Angie blush from his praise.

"I'd like to take all the credit, but Heidi and Robin love to talk about themselves and each other."

"It's more than that," he insisted. "It's like you understand the feminine psyche."

Angie pressed her lips together and her mood shifted subtly. "I should hope so," she said slowly. "I *am* a woman."

He was fully and painfully aware of that. "You know what I mean."

"Yes." She nodded, then rolled her shoulders back and thrust out her chin. "You're amazed that someone like me can understand how a woman thinks."

"That's not what I said at all. It's just that you're nothing like those women." When she was around, he was oblivious to anyone else.

"That's true." Angie suddenly stood up. Her face was pale and expressionless, as if she wore a mask. "I need to get going."

Did he say something wrong? He was trying to compliment her but he made a mess out of it. "What's the rush?"

"Personal stuff," she said, avoiding eye contact. "I'll see you around. Thanks for the kiss, er...coffee."

"It was my pleasure," he said. "Always."

6

"I'M OPEN!" ANGIE waved her hands in the air as she tried to get her basketball partner's attention. Tim, her opponent, bumped into her. Angie pushed back. The game was aggressive and close. She'd already gotten an elbow in the face during a jump ball. She gave as good as she got.

Angie was glad she didn't skip her weekly game. She needed the familiar sight of the dark green trees, the long stretches of thick grassy lawns and the faded basketball courts. She found comfort in watching the seniors on their benches, the kids running free and even the dog walkers, who tried to balance leashes, cell phones and coffee cups with only two hands. But most of all, she enjoyed being with her real friends. This was where she belonged.

She needed this, Angie decided as she wiped her sweaty hands against her long basketball shorts. It was good to take a break from dress fittings and bridesmaid meetings. And Cole. She definitely needed a break from him.

Angie frowned. She hadn't heard from him since the

day before, at the hospital. That was good. That was what she wanted. It took her a year to get over that guy and she didn't want to go through another Cole detox.

But how was she going to forget that kiss? Angie bit her lip as she fought back the memory of Cole's mouth against hers. The kiss started out soft and teasing. She tried to hold back but then his kiss grew demanding. Or maybe she had demanded more. There was a moment when she wasn't sure who was in charge. She had tried to resist, but his kisses were better than she remembered. His touch still excited her. She never responded as wildly with another man.

Tim blocked her and Angie shook her head, trying to get her head back into the game. She dodged and Tim tried to grab her oversize shirt but failed. She wasn't as tall as her basketball buddies, but she made up for it with speed. "C'mon, Steve!" she yelled as she ran next to the basket. "Give it to me."

"I'd throw it to you," Steve said as he tried to set up a difficult shot from the three-point line, "but I'm afraid you'll break a nail."

Angie smiled as the other guys laughed. "Why don't you come a little closer and I'll show you how strong my nails are."

"Yeah, right— Hey!" Steven complained as Patrick stole the basketball. "Foul!"

Angie watched as her best friend sank the ball in the basket. She groaned and dropped her shoulders in disappointment. "Steve, next time throw me the ball."

"It's much more fun teasing you," he said.

"Be careful," Angie warned. "You and I are walking together at the end of the wedding. I just may trip you."

Steve's eyes widened with horror. "You wouldn't dare."

She pushed her finger against his chest. "Don't tempt me."

"You don't have anything to worry about," Tim told Steve. "Angie has to wear high heels. She'll be too busy clinging onto you, never mind trying to trip you."

"Clinging? Not going to happen," Angie insisted as she made a face. "I've worn heels before."

Tim and Steve gave each other a look of disbelief. "She's going to take the whole procession down," Steve predicted to Tim. "It'll be one big pileup."

"A stack of dominos," Tim decided.

"I'm not listening." She pressed her hands over her ears. "La-la-la-la." She wouldn't tell them that the heels were a concern. She actually followed her mother's advice and had been practicing walking in her bridesmaid shoes. They were taller than anything she'd worn and she wasn't as graceful as she wished.

"Hey," Patrick said as he bounced the ball to Angie and jerked his head to the park entrance. "Is that Cole Foster?"

Oh, damn. She winced as she slowly turned to where Patrick indicated. Cole was walking through the city park and heading to the basketball courts. Her heart gave a jolt. He was dressed in a hoodie and jeans, warding off the cool Seattle breeze, but she remembered how strong and lean his body felt against hers.

"Yeah, that's him." she answered weakly as pleasure, dark and heavy, settled low in her pelvis. How did he find her? It wasn't as if he would remember her schedule.

Patrick placed his hands on his hips. "What is he doing here?"

"You want us to get rid of him?" Tim offered.

"Uh…no." Angie pressed her palms against the basketball. She dreaded having to tell her friends about Cole. They knew how much she had suffered when Cole left. She didn't talk about it but they had tried to keep life normal for her. They probably wouldn't believe she was back with him, but she couldn't tell them the whole truth. That this was merely pretend. Or at least, it was supposed to be. That kiss sure felt real.

"Really?" Steve asked. "We can do it. It's three of us against one of him."

"No!" she said sharply and gripped the basketball tighter. She knew Cole could handle any situation but she still felt very protective of him. She had worried about him when he had been on the force. Cole's colleagues had told her stories about his heroism. The idea of him hurt or in trouble had plagued her, but she had learned to trust that Cole wouldn't take any unnecessary risks. She had known that his top priority was being with her, safe and sound at the end of the day.

"What's going on?" Tim asked. "You're acting weird."

"I've been meaning to tell you guys." She cleared her throat and spoke quickly. "Cole is my wedding date."

"What?" Steve said in a squawk. "Is this a joke?"

"It's the funniest thing." She gave a nervous laugh and bent her head, concentrating on her dribbling technique. "I bumped into Cole and one thing led to another. And, I, uh…invited him."

"Have you lost your mind?" Patrick asked, his deep voice booming.

"One too many basketballs to the head," Tim muttered.

"You guys, it's fine." She held up a placating hand

as she watched Cole getting closer. "There are no hard feelings."

Patrick shook his head. "Well, *you* may not have them, but we do."

She tossed the basketball to the side and let it bounce away. "Patrick, I swear, do not—"

"Hey." Cole gave a nod as he stepped on the basketball court. She saw the caution flicker in his eyes as he saw her friends form a protective wall in front of her. "Haven't seen you guys for a while."

"Yeah," Tim said as he puffed out his chest. "Not since you dumped Angie and broke her heart."

"Tim!" She tried to step in front of Tim and Steve but they weren't budging.

"Now you're sniffing around her again?" Steve asked. "I don't like the sound of that."

"You have no say in the matter," Angie pointed out.

"I disagree," Steve said. "I don't stand by quietly when someone hurts my friend."

"I'm fine, you guys," Angie repeated. She jumped but couldn't see over their shoulders. "No harm done."

"Are you kidding?" Patrick looked back at her. "Cole played with your head. You don't date. You haven't looked at another guy since."

"Okay! That's enough." She jogged around her friends and held up her hands for them to stop. "I can take over now."

"We got your back," Tim told her. "If he's causing trouble, just let us know."

"Thank you." Angie pulled Cole's sleeve, silently encouraging him to walk away with her. "Ignore them," she said quietly. "They get a little aggressive but it's all show."

"Don't believe that for a second." He looked over his

shoulder and smiled at Tim's posturing. "Those guys would take a punch for you."

"And they know I would take one for them." Angie grimaced when she realized how unfeminine that sounded. If she wanted to remind Cole that she was a woman, then that was not the way to go.

Cole stopped when they were off the basketball court. "Is it true? That you don't date?"

Patrick and his big mouth! Angie felt the heat of embarrassment in her face. "He has a tendency to exaggerate when he's trying to make a point."

Cole looked in her eyes and then abruptly looked away. "I didn't mean to hurt you," he said solemnly.

"Yeah, I know." Angie began to fidget. She didn't want to discuss how he broke her heart or how she'd never be the same. She believed she had found someone who adored her for who she was. She wasn't sure why that wasn't true.

"I had some personal stuff to get through," Cole continued to explain. "I was hurting and the last thing I wanted to do was cause you pain. That's why I broke up with you but it turns out I hurt you, anyway."

"Personal stuff?" Angie asked, crossing her arms. "Too personal that you couldn't share with your girlfriend? I knew you were holding back."

Cole sighed and raked his hand through his hair. "I thought it was best to let you go than to drag you into it."

Angie stepped around him so her friends couldn't see her anger. "You know, you may think that sounds all noble, but it's not. It's an insult. Do you think I'm fragile? That I couldn't have understood or helped you?"

"It wasn't something I could share."

"And something you still don't feel like sharing. I get it." He clearly didn't want to tell her even though it had come between them. Was still between them. Cole was always private but this was too much. "Why are you here?" she asked abruptly. "I'm in the middle of something."

Cole hesitated. "I need a favor," he mumbled.

Angie clenched her jaw and slowly shook her head. She wanted to refuse. Or tell him she would do him the favor only when he confided about his personal problem. Although if she tried that, there was no guarantee that he would tell her the truth.

Maybe her friends were right to form a wall between her and Cole. All he had to do was show up and she got sucked back into his world. She was reluctant to tell him to leave yet she knew that was the smarter move.

But the sooner she helped him, the quicker he would get out of her life. She could stop thinking about him and be able to concentrate on the things that were important to her. "You are going to owe me so big after this wedding. What's the favor?"

Cole squeezed his eyes shut as if he knew he was pushing his luck with her. "I need the invitation list for the bachelorette party."

That wasn't the request she was expecting. "I don't think I can help you with that. I've never seen it and I didn't know many people at the party. Cheryl was in charge of all that."

"Do you think you can get it from her?" Cole asked. "I want to see if anyone else from Heidi's past was at the party. There may have been other sorority sisters who had a grudge against her."

She considered the best way to approach Brittany's assistant with a request. The woman looked sweet and friendly but Angie had seen during the wedding preparations that Cheryl could be stubborn. "I can call her or drop by Brittany's office, but I don't even have a reason to ask for the guest list."

"You'll come up with something." He reached out and wrapped his fingers around her wrist. "I know it."

She was reluctant to pull away but she was sure he could feel her racing pulse under his touch. "Your faith in my abilities is misplaced."

"No way." He gradually brought her close until they almost touched. "I've seen you finish a marathon when you had nothing left. I've seen you build your business from nothing to a success. I've even seen you win an argument with your mother. You will come up with a brilliant excuse."

"Fine," she reluctantly agreed. She hated how much pleasure she felt when she saw his appreciative smile. "But you're coming with me. If I talk myself into a corner, you'll have to get me out."

"I'm with you all the way."

Yeah, right. Angie broke from his hold. *We'll see about that.*

COLE STOOD AT Angie's side as they visited Brittany's office. The suite was probably as big as his agency but he still felt claustrophobic. The dark green walls in the front room made the place feel smaller. The floor was painted in black-and-white stripes and the bookshelves were crammed with magazines and catalogs.

He felt like a giant standing next to the delicate furniture. Cole wrinkled his nose and glanced at Angie. How could she chat effortlessly with the assistant and not keel over from the headache-inducing scented candles?

"I'm sorry?" Cheryl asked as she set down a pile of pastel—and probably scented—files. "You want to do what?"

"I want to get a hold of everyone from the bachelorette party and see if they'd like to chip in for a special gift for Brittany," Angie replied with a bright smile. "It would make her feel better, like the bridal spa did. And what with Heidi in the hospital and all. Cole, don't you think Brittany needs a little pampering?"

"Absolutely." But what the heck was a bridal spa? He felt as if he were in a different land, where they spoke a foreign language.

Cheryl gave him a cursory look. It was clear she didn't understand why he was accompanying Angie. It was time to sell the adoring-lover routine but Cole was slightly worried. He had gotten carried away when he kissed Angie the last time and she'd been pushing back ever since. Would she automatically reject his touch?

He had never taken Angie's affection for granted. He always knew that if he reached out his hand she would take it in hers. She knew how to arouse and how to comfort him with a simple touch. She could tease him during the day and at night she held him in her sleep. He'd never felt alone when she was in his life.

Cole hesitated before curling his arm around Angie's waist. He didn't realize he was holding his breath until she instantly leaned into his embrace.

"What's the special gift?" Cheryl asked Angie. She said it with nonchalance, but there was something about her tone. As if she expected Angie to want her approval.

"Uh...it's, uh..." Angie looked up at him.

He saw the flicker of uncertainty in Angie's brown eyes. "For the honeymoon," he stated.

She flashed him a grateful smile. "Yes, a thoughtful gift for their wedding night."

"Something that both the bride and groom will enjoy," he added.

Cheryl chose to ignore him. "That's really sweet of you, Angie, but I can't give out the guest list. A lot of her clients are on there."

"I understand, but—"

He pressed his fingers against Angie's waist. He had done a lot of legwork in his past career to know when someone was going to be helpful or not. No one could persuade Cheryl to hand over that list.

"And I can't let someone they don't know have access to it," Cheryl explained cheerfully, but he heard the firmness in her voice.

"What if I—"

"And, to be honest," Cheryl interrupted with a smile, "I don't think they would appreciate being hit up for more money. It's a great idea, but it could create a negative feeling."

He felt Angie's shoulders slump in defeat. "You're right."

"But if you want to give Brittany a gift for her wedding night, I'll make sure it's in the honeymoon suite." Cheryl rose from behind her desk. Cole knew it was a move to end this meeting.

"Thank you. I'll let you know." She turned to him. "Let's go."

"See you later." He saluted Cheryl with a wave but the woman continued to ignore him.

He opened the door for Angie and she stopped at the threshold. "Cheryl, have there been any updates on Heidi?"

Cheryl pressed her lips. "She's out of the hospital

but she can't be part of the bridal party. Doctor's orders. It's a disaster."

Angie clucked her tongue. "Poor Heidi. She was so looking forward to it."

"I couldn't tell by the way she kept complaining about the work," Cheryl said. "Robin will be maid of honor. Honestly, I don't think she's up for the job."

"Fortunately, Robin and Brittany have you to help," Angie said sincerely.

Cole saw the anger and irritation flash in Cheryl's eyes. "It's overwhelming but I want Brittany to have a perfect wedding."

"Will Heidi be at the ceremony at least?" he asked. He muffled a grunt when Angie dug her elbow in his side.

"She doesn't know yet." Cheryl looked at him with open suspicion. "Why?"

"Just wondering," Angie answered for him. She grabbed his hand and led him out the door.

"Well, that didn't work at all," Angie whispered the minute he closed the door behind them. She let go of his hand once they passed the window to Brittany's office and walked ahead of him to the parking lot.

"It was a long shot. We're working under the assumption that someone tried to hurt Heidi because of the past. As far as we know, the only people who knew her were Brittany, Robin and the sorority sisters who attended the party.

"But why wait and do it in such a public place? And why now?" Angie asked.

"I don't know but I have to find out. This may have something to do with her past, but what if it's about something that's going on in her life now? What if she hasn't changed and her family can't accept that?"

"You're putting too much responsibility on yourself," Angie said. "There is only so much you can do."

"If Heidi gets back together with her family only to get kicked out again, it'll be devastating." He knew what it was like to hope for a reconciliation only to have everything fall apart. To discover that your worst-case scenario was nothing compared to what actually happened. "I want to prevent it. I can if I have enough information."

"You will," Angie promised. "You found Heidi, you did the surveillance and now you're looking into the accident when no one else is. If there is any kind of evidence, you will find it."

"I wonder why Cheryl wouldn't give us the list," he said. "You think she's hiding something?"

"No, that list represents Brittany's business. She has to protect it. I think I would do the same. It took me years to build up my list of clients and I would want to maintain their privacy. Cheryl's just doing her job."

"I wish I had a Cheryl working for me," Cole said. There were times when he could use any help he could get. But the only person he wanted in his corner was Angie. "Except I would want someone that didn't give me the evil eye."

"Ah, you noticed that, too? Maybe she doesn't approve of strippers." She paused as they stepped out onto the parking lot. There was a light drizzle of rain that they ignored as the drops danced on the cars and rippled puddles on the pavement. "I'm sorry I didn't get that list. I should have come up with a better story."

"Hey, it was a good one." Cole wanted to comfort her. He gathered her in his arms and held her close. "We'll come up with something else."

Angie's shoulders stiffened and she stepped out of

his embrace. "Cole, you don't have to act love-struck. No one is watching."

"That's—" He bit back the words as the hurt cut through him. She was right. He had stepped out of line and blurred pretend with reality. "Sorry, Angie. It won't happen again. I promise."

7

COLE LEANED BACK in his chair and stared at the computer screen. He had been trying to write his report on Heidi but he wasn't getting far. All he could think about was Angie.

They were once a good team. It didn't matter if they had been enjoying a night out or had suffered through the worst weekend getaway—they had faced each moment as partners. In the beginning it had made him uncomfortable. He did better alone.

The last people he had relied on were his mom and stepdad. Only their love had been conditional. No matter how much he tried to do better, *be* better, it wasn't good enough. They had deserted him when he needed them the most.

When he was with Angie, he had tried his best. He wanted it so much for them to work. He tried to hide the darkness but she seemed to know and understand. She didn't push, but most importantly, she never pulled away. Even when she saw him at his worst, she was there at his side.

Which was why it stung when Angie pulled out of his arms in the parking lot.

He didn't touch her because he thought someone was watching. He wasn't thinking about his surroundings at all. He had simply longed for the connection they once shared.

It was his fault and he deserved to have her shut him down. He had gotten carried away in the role and slipped back into a time when he could hold her. Show his claim with a possessive touch. But Angie wasn't his anymore.

Cole heard the outer door to his office open. He sat up straight and listened to the door close quietly. That was strange. He didn't get many walk-ins.

"Hello?" The deep male voice echoed in the waiting area.

Cole dragged his hands over his face and sighed before he stood and left his tiny office. He should have known Patrick would not let this matter rest but he didn't feel like dealing with it right now.

"Patrick," he greeted the other man, noticing his wet hair and soaked coat. There were dark patches on Patrick's shoes and jeans that indicated he'd stepped into a deep puddle. What they said was true, Cole decided. No one in Seattle owned an umbrella. "What brings you here?"

He glared at Cole and shook his head as the water sprayed from his drenched hair. "I want some answers."

Cole should have known he wasn't going to get out of this. "Sure. Sit down."

"No, thanks. It won't be necessary." Patrick braced his legs and crossed his arms. "This will be very short."

Cole waited. In the past, he and Patrick tolerated each other. They were both territorial about Angie. It took a while before Cole realized Patrick had no romantic interest in Angie. He never understood that. Angie was the most fascinating and sensual woman he'd ever met but her friends saw her as one of the guys.

At first he thought it was unusual that Angie's closest friends were men. He didn't like it. But he never complained or asked that she didn't hang around those guys. He didn't want to make it a competition, especially since he had a feeling he would lose. It took him a few months before he realized he was being ridiculous.

Unlike the women he had dated in the past, Angie wasn't flirty or suggestive with other men. She didn't want to make him jealous. Instead, she went out of her way to make him feel like he was the most important man in her life.

"Don't mess with Angie and don't mess with this wedding," Patrick warned.

"I don't plan to do either." But his original plan was unraveling quickly. All he wanted to do was find Heidi and determine if she still had a substance abuse problem. Now he was tangled again in Angie's life, resurrecting feelings and struggling between make-believe and reality.

"Brittany really needs this wedding to be perfect," Patrick insisted. He suddenly looked weary. "She is so stressed out that she's breaking out in hives. The last thing I need is for you to bring more drama to the situation."

"Okay." Unlike the rest of the bridal party, the wedding was the least of his concerns. All he wanted was to find out what happened to the maid of honor.

"I don't know why you're back in Angie's life, but I don't like it," he said. "It can only mean trouble."

Cole stood very still. Patrick didn't know the truth.

After what happened on the basketball court, he was sure Angie would tell her best friend the real reason they were together. Did she keep his secret to protect him or to keep Patrick from worrying?

"I'm sure you've discussed this with Angie," Cole said. Was that why Angie pulled away from him? Did Patrick express the many reasons he thought they shouldn't be together? Cole didn't doubt that the list was a long one.

"I did, but she's not listening." He made a face that Cole understood. Angie could be very stubborn. "She always had a soft spot where you were concerned. But I don't. And I'm not going to let you hurt her a second time."

"I don't want to hurt her." Why did everyone think he didn't have her best interest at heart? "I care about her more than anybody."

"And look at where that got her. She was ready to move in with you." Patrick shook his head with disbelief. "She was afraid you'd say no, but she went for it, anyway."

Angie had been nervous? He would never have known. She seemed almost casual when she suggested they move in together. But it had been a big deal for him. He had wanted to jump at the offer but experience taught him to hold back. He made a decision to revisit his past instead and was still reeling from that trip down memory lane.

"And you couldn't get away fast enough." Patrick looked at him with disgust. "I told her it was a bad idea."

"I loved Angie but I couldn't live with her." He realized how that sounded. Angie wasn't the problem; he was. Cole was tempted to explain, but that would require revealing too much. "It would never have worked."

"You loved her?" Patrick gave a harsh bark of laughter. "You have a funny way of showing it."

"It doesn't matter now," Cole said, forcing back the anger. He learned long ago not to show how much someone meant to him. That knowledge would be used against him. "I messed up and she's won't give me another chance. She'll drop me once this wedding is over."

"Good." Patrick's tone was low and emphatic. "She needs to move on and stop listening to the gossip."

Gossip? He couldn't imagine anyone judging Angie. That could only mean he was the subject. "What gossip? Was it about Angie and me?"

"I'm not getting into it." Patrick turned and headed for the door.

"You came here and started this," Cole reminded him. He needed to know what was said to Angie. "What were they saying?"

Patrick faced him and scoffed. "There was some talk about why you broke up with Angie."

His gut twisted. That was impossible. No one knew about his family life around here. They didn't know about his history, but maybe that didn't matter. People made assumptions when they didn't know the truth.

Patrick's gaze slid away. "Rumor was you wanted someone hotter."

Cole slowly blinked. "Excuse me?"

"You wanted a hotter girlfriend. Someone—" he motioned at his chest "—you know. Sexier. Girlier." He dropped his hands. "A lot of people told Angie that she lost you because she wasn't doing enough to keep you interested."

"I… *What?*" How could anyone think that? Angie was fun, sexy and had a wild streak that left him breathless. She was uninhibited in bed and demonstrated a woman could be strong and feminine.

Patrick shrugged and took a few steps to the door. He was clearly uncomfortable with this discussion. "I'm only repeating what I heard. I didn't say I believed it."

"Good, because that is the furthest thing from the truth. Angie is more than beautiful. She's amazing and—"

He held up his hand. "Dude, I really don't want to hear it."

"Why would she think that?" Was it something he said or did? But what? He didn't feel that way about her at all.

"She's been told that crap for years," Patrick said. "Angie's different from the women around here. Always has been. She got teased a lot about that at school until she started kicking ass in sports."

Was that why she was shutting him out? Was it because she believed he was faking his attraction? He thought she complained because it reminded her of their past. Could it be because she felt insecure about her sex appeal?

"And remember," Patrick said, "you didn't hear it from me."

Cole nodded absently, trying to think of a time when Angie had felt shy with him. "And I promise, I'm not going to cause any problems with Angie and the wedding."

"We'll see about that," Patrick muttered as he left the office. "I won't hesitate to kick you out of the church."

"I've been warned." And he deserved to get banned from the ceremony if he tried to sabotage the wedding.

But right now he had more pressing matters. He had to clear up these lies with Angie. Right now. He didn't want her to think for another moment that she wasn't good enough for him.

Didn't she realize that it was the other way around?

Cole stood by Angie's apartment door and flexed his hands. He looked around and counted all of the security features that were lacking in her hallway. He hated that she chose to live in a renovated factory in one of the most run-down neighborhoods. But he had to admit that the old brick building suited her. The large arched windows would welcome the rare sunshine and the oddly shaped studio apartment was the perfect backdrop for her flea-market finds and mismatched furniture.

The only thing that didn't fit in her home, her life, was him. He took a step back, prepared to abandon this idea. Dipping his head, he drew all the courage he had and knocked on the door.

He really didn't think this through, Cole decided as he stared at the heavy, plain brown door. He wasn't sure what he was going to say. How was he supposed to erase a year of hurt with a few words? He couldn't.

He heard the scratch of the lock. His heart thudded against his ribs as the door swung open. Cole's eyes widened as he watched a sleepy Angie stumble into the lit hallway.

Her thick black hair was tousled and cascaded past her shoulders. His fingers itched to sink into the soft waves and draw her close to him.

Angie glared. Her face was soft from sleep. She really was a natural beauty. She didn't need anything to highlight her big brown eyes or her full pink lips.

His mouth dropped open as he stared at her clothes. Her small breasts were pressed against her thin camisole. The top was almost sheer and he could see her nipples through the thin white fabric. The black boyshorts accentuated her sleek lines and incredible legs.

"Do you always answer the door like that?" he asked gruffly.

"Did you come all the way to my home to comment on my sleepwear?" she asked as she rubbed her bleary eyes.

"No." His voice sounded strangled to his ears. He liked what she wore a little too much. She didn't need frilly nighties or barely there lingerie to capture his attention. The camisole and shorts were more her style and showed off her sexy and athletic body.

"What do you want, Cole?" Angie flipped her long black hair away from her face. "Another favor?"

Yeah, and it was huge. He wanted her to forgive him. Forget that he left her. Welcome him back into her bed and in her life.

"What could possibly be so important at this time at night?" she asked.

He checked his watch. "It's ten-thirty."

She groaned. "That's the middle of the night for me."

That was true, Cole thought as he bit back a smile. As a personal trainer, Angie had to get up before dawn to meet with her clients. She had always apologized for her early hours, but he didn't mind. He wasn't looking for nights in dance clubs and bars when he could be alone with her.

"Is this about your case?" she asked. "The wedding

is in three days and then everybody goes home. I don't think there's much more you can do."

He could lie and say he was here for the case. But he had used his assignment as an excuse to get closer. He wasn't going to hide behind his job. He had been too private and guarded in the past. It protected him but not Angie. She believed in what other people said. He won't let that happen again.

"I made a mistake."

Angie frowned. "About Heidi's accident?"

"No, I meant about us." He took a deep breath. "I made a mistake breaking up with you. It's my biggest regret."

She looked down at her bare feet. "What brought this on?"

"You think I'm overplaying the role as your on-again boyfriend. You're right." His words were choppy. He wished he could be a smooth talker but it was difficult getting his feelings across. "Being together reminds me what I've lost. I miss being with you."

Angie's eyes narrowed and her mouth tightened. "You knew what you were giving up when you walked away."

He should have known he wouldn't get any sympathy from her. "You suggested we move in together and I panicked." It wasn't the whole truth. There was so much more to it but he didn't feel safe in revealing it all.

"That's why? Seriously?" She stood straight and grasped the door handle, ready to slam it in his face. "I mentioned it once. It's not like I tried to give you a hard sell."

"I felt that if we lived together, you would see the sides of me that aren't so—" he gritted his teeth and pushed the word out "—loveable. You wouldn't like what you saw."

"I never thought you were perfect."

"You would have grown to hate me." Like his family did. He had gotten in the way of what they always wanted. "I thought it was best to end things so you had a chance to find someone better. Someone you could really love."

Angie slowly shook her head. "You shouldn't have done that."

Cole nervously rubbed the back of his neck. "I know that now. I wish I'd never made that mistake and been the boyfriend you needed."

"You were the boyfriend I wanted but your attitude changed in that last month." Her voice carried a hint of the confusion and hurt from that time. "I had loved you, Cole. Didn't you see that?"

He was stunned. His heart stopped and his ears started to buzz. The room kind of slanted as his whole world went off balance. *"You loved me?"*

Angie blushed but she held his gaze. "Why are you so surprised? I wouldn't have talked about moving in otherwise."

She loved him. She had never said those words before. All he wanted was Angie's love but he didn't think he had it. He had left because he didn't think he could earn her love. Now he realized he had thrown it away.

The regret and loss weighed heavily on him. He felt like he needed to hold on to something before he slid down to the ground. He wanted to lean against Angie and hold on to her until his world righted itself.

She had loved him. Once. How did she feel about

him now? No, he didn't want to ask that question. What if she couldn't love him again? What if he couldn't get her back?

He'd take whatever she was willing to give as long as she didn't shut him out. Cole took a step closer. "Invite me in," he said in a husky voice.

Angie swallowed roughly. "That's not a good idea."

"It's a very good idea. I've been thinking about it and so have you." When she didn't deny it, he boldly took a step closer. "I can't stop thinking about you. How good we were together."

"It's best if we don't try to recapture what we once had," she whispered.

He wanted what they once had. Angie was the only one who had cracked the protective wall around him. She was the only person he could trust and the only woman who could turn him into knots. The power she had over him was at times troubling. There was so much he kept to himself because he knew from experience that knowledge was power. But as their relationship grew stronger, he noticed that he was sharing more about himself and his life with her. It was scary and at the same time deeply gratifying. He'd never had anything like it and he never would again.

He knew they couldn't get what they had. Too much time had passed. Too much distance. But he wanted her back. He was willing to work toward something different. Something better. He wanted a fresh start.

Cole's body grazed hers. He wanted to demonstrate how much he missed her. How much he loved her. "Let me in."

She stared at him with wide eyes. "This is insane."

Cole lowered his head and brushed his mouth

against hers. Angie's lips clung to his. Hope squeezed his chest when she didn't pull away. He gathered her close, stepped into her apartment and kicked the door behind him.

8

ANGIE PRESSED COLE against the door. Her apartment was dark and quiet but her mind was a whirlwind. She'd wanted this since she had seen him on stage. His lap dance had invaded her dreams. It had been so long since she had felt aroused. Felt anything for a man. It was sharp and instant, making her movements clumsy as the lust poured through her veins.

A sense of urgency pulsed through her but Cole was in no rush. He savored her mouth with thorough kisses. He teased her with his tongue, darting the tip along her reddened lips before plunging into her mouth, only to withdraw.

She shivered when she felt his large, rough hands slide down her back. She leaned into Cole, arching her spine as he trailed his hands down to her bottom. He squeezed hard and she growled in the back of her throat.

Angie froze. She shouldn't do that. The last thing she needed to remind Cole was how unladylike she was in the bedroom.

She rubbed her body restlessly against him. She

wanted to tear off his clothes and climb onto his naked body. She flattened her hands against his chest and felt the heavy and uneven beat of his heart. She didn't want to follow his lead and go slow. She needed this to be hard and fast. Next time they could have a leisurely exploration.

Next time. The words swirled in her head and she stopped rocking her hips against Cole. There would be no next time. Nothing had really changed. He said he missed her. He missed this.

This was sex.

Angie hesitated as the realization hit. Should she grab this opportunity or kick him out? Sex with Cole was once about love and connecting two souls. She had shared everything with him when they were in bed. Now he was offering this one night. There was no promise of a future yet she wanted more. It wasn't enough.

But it was more than she had yesterday...

She should end this. One more kiss and she would break away. Cole gently cupped the back of her head and suckled her lips. She felt the pull to her core. One more kiss, she decided. And it would be the last one. The last time she shared a kiss—shared anything— with Cole Foster.

Cole broke the kiss and pressed his mouth against her ear. "You have no idea what you're doing to me."

She knew. His skin was hot and his raspy breath couldn't hide his excitement. She felt his erection pressing against her. His penis was hard and thick. Angie moaned with anticipation.

A thought wafted through her mind like smoke. They should stop now. Pull away before they reached the point of no return.

Cole placed his hands on her hips and turned her around. The move was so sudden that she fell back against him. He burrowed his face in her hair as he dipped his hand lower.

Angie's breath staggered from her throat as Cole boldly cupped her sex. She instinctively flattened her hand against his.

"Angie." He dragged her name out in a rough whisper. "Let me touch you." His fingers flexed. "Please you."

She bit her lip as the erotic memories crashed over her. Cole not only knew how to satisfy her, but he also gave her maximum pleasure. He was generous and imaginative. Strong and loving. With one intimate touch, he could make her believe that they were made for each other.

But would she feel the same tonight? He didn't love her. He didn't want to share a future or even a home. All he wanted was to share a bed. Would this one time taint those special memories? Was she willing to risk feeling empty and alone for a shadow of what they used to share?

Cole delved his other hand beneath her camisole and covered her breast. He lightly pinched her stiff nipple as he stroked the folds of her sex with his other hand.

Yes, she was willing. Angie rested her head against his broad shoulder as her knees threatened to buckle. *Yes,* she mouthed in the darkness as she pressed the heel of her palm against his hand. She bucked against him. *Yes.*

"Take off my clothes," Angie ordered softly.

"Patience," he said.

She frowned. This was not a time to be patient. She hadn't been able to see Cole, touch him, or hear his groans of satisfaction for a year. She needed to feel his skin on hers with no barriers. No restrictions. Angie grabbed the hem of her camisole.

"No." Cole gave a warning nip to her earlobe. "I'm in charge."

Angie's fingers dug into the cotton as she considered her next move. She should have known. Last time she had been demanding and insatiable. She hadn't held anything back, confident that Cole wanted her just as much. That he was turned on by her assertiveness.

"Let me take care of you." Cole's voice was low and mesmerizing. "I know what you like." He pressed his fingertip against her throbbing clit.

"But…" Pleasure rippled lightly through her.

"I'll give you anything you want." His voice was urgent with need.

He would give her anything…as long as he was in charge. As long as she surrendered. She shouldn't care, Angie decided as she closed her eyes. She hadn't always been brazen in bed. Not until she had felt secure with Cole.

And that had been a mistake. She wouldn't repeat it again. If she held back, if she didn't follow every animal instinct or reckless impulse, she could have her ex-boyfriend for one more night.

Angie gradually let go of her shirt and was rewarded with Cole's sigh. She looped her hands over his shoulders. Now she was open to his touch, giving him total control. It shouldn't make her so nervous.

Cole grasped her jaw and tilted her head toward him. She felt the kick of power at how his fingers trembled against her chin. But his kiss was confident and demanding as he claimed her mouth.

Her skin tingled as the shameless need built inside

her. She swallowed back a keening cry as she writhed against his hand. The pleasure promised to be intense. Her heart raced as her stomach twisted with wild expectation.

Angie wished Cole would stop teasing her. She wanted to turn around, strip him bare and take over. But that would put a stop to everything. There was only one thing she could do.

"Please," she said in a jagged breath.

She bucked when Cole squeezed her nipple while also pressing against her swollen bud. The pleasure exploded inside her. Her mind shut down and she cried out. Angie slumped forward, her legs going limp. Cole caught her and gathered her close.

She was dimly aware of him carrying her. His shirt pressed against her cheek and she heard his heartbeat close to her ear. Her chest rose and fell as her muscles shook slightly. Her skin felt hot and her clothes were too confining.

Cole lowered her onto her warm, welcoming bed. She reached out for him and he wrapped his hands around hers. "First I need to find the light."

Something close to panic gripped her chest. "No," she said. "No lights."

She felt Cole's pause. "Why not?"

Angie didn't know how to explain it. They had been lovers but this time it was different. This time she knew she wasn't feminine enough for him. She lacked big breasts and generous hips. She didn't have anything sexy to wear that could heighten his pleasure before he unwrapped her like a present.

She was the same person he left a year ago. A little wiser and more cautious this time around. She wasn't going to be free and uninhibited with him. Men wanted a little mystery. A fantasy.

"Angie?"

She drew his head down and kissed him. It was meant to distract him from the light but it only managed to lower her guard. She instinctively tangled her legs with his. His jeans were scratchy against her bare skin. She was tempted to roll over, straddle Cole and shuck off his clothes.

Her body must have signaled her intent. Cole wrapped his fingers around her wrists and held her hands over her head. Her first instinct was to wrestle for control. Roll him under her and tease him with her mouth and hands. Drive him wild until he was begging for release.

Cole had loved that. Or so she thought.

He kissed a trail down her throat and circled the tip of his tongue against her trembling pulse point. She rolled her hips in response and bumped against his rock-hard penis. Her flesh clenched with desperate need. "Take off your clothes," she insisted. She didn't care how bossy she sounded—she wanted him naked now.

"You first," he said with his mouth pressed against her shoulder. She gasped with appreciation as he dragged the camisole strap down with his teeth. Angie couldn't stop herself from thrusting her breast to his mouth.

Her nipples stung and she couldn't remain still. She wiggled her hips against Cole and her legs locked behind his. She fought for self-control until he took her breast in his mouth. Angie surrendered to his touch.

She allowed her legs to drop as she sinuously arched her back. Her short, choppy breaths mingled with his.

He drew sharply on her nipple and let go of her hands so he could fondle her breasts. His touch grew increasingly impatient as his restraint started to crumble.

Angie grabbed the back of his head, her fingertips tangled in his thick hair. Sweat bathed her skin as the heat billowed inside her.

Cole slid her boyshorts down her legs. She kicked them off as he settled between her thighs.

"Wait," he said hoarsely. She heard the metallic sound of his zipper and the rustle of his clothes. His shoes hit the floor. She lowered her hands onto the bed, clutching the sheets, as she held back from shoving his jeans off him.

She licked her swollen lips, excitement squeezing her lungs, as he placed his firm hands on her thighs. Angie took a deep breath when she felt the tip of his penis pressing against her. Her sharp intake echoed in her ears as Cole surged forward.

Angie went still for a brief moment as her body yielded to his. Blood roared in her ears as her skin flushed. Immediately, she tilted her hips and drew him in more.

Cole's thrusts were strong and steady. His hands were everywhere. Her stomach fluttered from his gentle, clumsy caress and her nipples tightened as he massaged her breasts.

Her heart skipped a beat when he stroked her hair before drawing his fingertips along her cheek. He placed his thumb against her chin, guiding her mouth open before he kissed her hard.

His kiss was possessive. Elemental. He was reminding her of his claim. And it triggered something primal inside her. Angie wrapped her arms and legs tightly against him and rolled them over.

Now she straddled Cole. He didn't seem to mind. She couldn't see his face but she heard snatches of his encouraging words. His fingers pressed into her hips, clearly approving of her frenetic pace.

She tore off her camisole and tossed it away. Angie flattened her hands on his chest, twisting his shirt in between her fingers as she followed an ancient rhythm. Her hair fell in her face, her skin felt like it was going to burst open and the desire coiling deep in her pelvis sprang wildly.

Her muscles locked and her body stilled as she climaxed. It stole her breath and she felt as if she were falling. She held on to Cole, grinding her hips against his hurried thrusts. She tumbled against him just as she heard his hoarse cry of release.

She lay next to him, her face pressed against his, as she struggled for her next breath. As she closed her eyes, Angie realized that nostalgia had played with her memory.

Sex with Cole was better than she had remembered.

COLE DIDN'T WANT to move. Angie was curled around him, soft and naked. She was his for the night and he wanted to hold on to this moment. He waited until Angie had fallen asleep before he changed positions. She didn't make a sound of complaint when he turned over and laid her tenderly on her pillow.

He wanted to stay with her. In the past he would toss the blanket over them to keep the world at bay and hold her all night. Those quiet minutes always meant a lot to him. Too much. Angie had made him feel special and wanted. She had made him feel as if he had found home.

He felt that tonight. He had been hesitant to embrace the feeling because he knew he couldn't hold on to it. He knew it wasn't real. They weren't a couple anymore and he needed to remember that. If he fell for the illusion, it would break him and he wouldn't be able to recover.

He reluctantly got out of bed and tucked the blanket over Angie. He tripped over his shoe and winced. Cole was about to turn on the bedside lamp but stopped as his fingertips brushed against the switch.

Why didn't Angie want the light on? That was unusual. She was not shy when it came to sex. In fact, she was the opposite. He loved that about her, but tonight he wanted to make it all about her pleasure. Why did she want it dark? Was she ashamed that she had fallen back in bed with him? Or did she still believe in the gossip that he didn't find her sexy enough?

He was going to fix that, Cole decided as he grabbed his jeans and yanked them on. He wasn't sure how he could prove his desire. Wasn't it already obvious? He was always aware of Angie and constantly dragging his gaze away only to find he was still staring at her.

And these days he couldn't stop touching her. Cole sighed as he picked up his shoes. He had found every excuse to hold her hand or touch her hair. And if he wasn't doing either of those things, he was likely touching her back to guide her as they walked. She didn't say anything when he placed his hand on her shoulder or waist. Did she know it was his way of showing the world that Angie was still his?

Now if only Angie felt the same, Cole thought as he made his way to the door in the dark. If only she wanted him back. She had loved him once. Could she fall in love with him again?

Cole flattened his hand on the door and looked over

at Angie. Would she welcome him back into her life or would she think this was all for appearances' sake? That he was doing all this for his case.

He shouldn't consider whether or not he could get Angie back. History had proven that it would not work in his favor. A year ago he had searched for his mother and stepfather and contacted them. The people who should automatically love and care about him rejected him again.

Still, Angie was different. She had accepted him even though he held back. If he wanted to have a fresh start with Angie, it had to begin now. Cole relocked the door and turned around. He slowly padded back to bed—back to Angie—as he shed his clothes. From now on, he was going to give everything he had to her. And pray that it was enough.

9

COLE FROWNED WHEN he heard an insistent buzzing sound. He rolled over and opened his eyes. He blinked when he saw the glass chandelier above him. Slowly sitting up, he noticed the sunlight streaming through the windows. He smiled contentedly when he saw the exposed brick walls and eclectic furniture. Everything in Angie's studio apartment reflected her personality.

Looking beside him, Cole found Angie still asleep. Her long black hair fanned against her colorful pillow and partially hid her face. The patchwork blanket had slid down to her waist, revealing her athletic body and firm breasts. He was tempted to lie back down and cradle her against his bare chest.

He heard the buzzing noise again. Cole glanced over at the bedside table and saw Angie's cell phone vibrate. He knew it would be her mother calling even before he could see the image of the older woman on the tiny, lit-up screen.

He smiled when he saw the casual snapshot of Angie's mother, glamorous as usual. She wasn't the kind of mother Cole had wished for growing up when he watched TV sitcoms. Angie's mother didn't bake or sew, although she certainly made sure her two sons and daughter had been fed and clothed, and were safe. Her first priority would always be her husband but she was also a constant presence in her children's lives. Sometimes a little too involved, according to her children. Angie had no idea how lucky she was that her parents even cared.

"Angie," Cole said as he shook her arm. "You need to wake up."

"Five more minutes," she mumbled. He was about to try again when he felt Angie's arm tighten. Cole knew she was suddenly and fully awake. She was now realizing that what happened last night was real and not a fantasy.

"Your mom is calling," he told her.

Angie reached for the blanket and dragged it up to her chin. "Ignore it."

"She's been calling. You know how worried she gets when you don't answer." He knew how this would play out and he liked how it never varied, even when her mother was angry with Angie. "If you don't answer, she'll make your dad call. And then your brothers."

"I'll call her back later," Angie said as she curled deeper into her pillow.

"If you don't answer it, I will." And he knew the havoc that would cause.

Angie bolted up and grabbed the phone. She glared at him while she carefully wound the blanket around her body. "Hey, Mom," she said, her voice rough from sleep. "Can I call you back?"

He knew that wasn't going to happen. Cole smiled when he heard Angie's sigh as she tucked the phone more comfortably next to her ear. He hadn't been around the Lawson household for a year, but he still understood the natural rhythms and the rules they lived by. The close ties and predictability drove Angie crazy, but he had secretly yearned for it.

He didn't idealize Angie's family. The Lawsons were loud and they didn't always get along, but the family offered solid support for each other. That was something he didn't have when he was growing up but he got it from the Lawsons. They had included him in their family with such speed that it had embarrassed Angie and it had made him nervous. He saw it as a privilege and a gift, but unlike Angie and her brothers, it was not given to him unconditionally.

Cole lay back down and got an unobstructed view of her strong and naked back. He was about to reach out and stroke his fingers down her spine when he noticed how she stiffened. It was as if Angie were on guard and sensing danger.

"Yes," she said tightly. "Cole is my date for the wedding. How did you know?"

Cole's chuckle was rewarded with the sharp swipe of her hand gesturing him to remain quiet. He didn't think it was necessary. When was Angie going to learn that she could not hide anything from her mother?

"No," she said firmly to her mother, "it doesn't mean anything…. No, it doesn't. I needed a date to the wedding and Cole was available."

He found it interesting that she wasn't telling her mother the real reason. But he also refused to think that this meant something. Did she worry that they had taken the pretense too far? He would prove to her that this was very real.

"No, there is nothing to discuss…. He's just returning a favor. No, you are not inviting him over for the family dinner. Mom…Mom?" She huffed and waved her hand in the air in surrender. "I give up. Do what you want. I have to go. 'Bye."

"I don't remember you being this grumpy in the morning," Cole said as he watched her end the call and toss the cell phone back onto the bedside table.

Angie tucked her knees to her chest. "If she calls you over for the Sunday dinner, don't accept."

"But I love those dinners," he teased. It had taken a while for him to get used to the chaotic meals and lively arguments with Angie's dad and brothers. They were casual, fun, and he felt like he was part of the family.

Angie reached over the bed and yanked her discarded camisole from the floor. "Do you really want to be interrogated by my mother?"

"I survived the first time." He laced his hands beneath his head and smiled with pride. "In fact, I passed with flying colors. She said I was a keeper." That casual comment had meant a lot to him.

"She is so embarrassing," Angie muttered as she put on her top. "I know you think she's adorable, but that's probably because you miss having your mother around."

Cole wasn't paying attention anymore. Angie's voice faded as she pulled on her clothes while listing the reasons why her mother drove her crazy. His heart began to thump and dread twisted his stomach. Cole battled back the nauseating fear. If he were going to stop holding back and start sharing, he had to do it now.

He looked down at the bedsheet. "I have a mother."

Angie stopped moving and stared at him. "I'm sorry, what?"

Cole forced himself to look at Angie. She seemed

stunned. "My mother is still alive," he said. "So is my stepdad."

Anger flashed in her eyes. Her mouth opened and closed. "You told me they were dead. You said you didn't have parents."

He rubbed the back of his neck as the shame clawed at him. "They stopped being my parents years ago, but they are still alive." Still married. Still a family without him. "I just thought you should know."

"You just…" She pressed her lips together into a stern line. "Of all the…"

Cole closed his eyes. He should have kept his mouth shut.

COLE LIED TO HER. *His parents were alive.* The words kept repeating in her mind. The hurt and surprise had reverberated inside her and she'd followed her first instinct to sprint for the bathroom. She felt betrayed and she didn't think she could control her wild emotions.

She had taken her time in the shower and changing her clothes, hoping Cole would have gotten the idea and slither out of her apartment and far, far away from her. Instead, he stayed. She'd seen the determined, almost defiant look in his eyes and she knew she was in for a battle. Angie had immediately scooped up her keys and walked out of the apartment, only to have Cole follow her.

Cole lied to her. His parents were alive. Angie glanced up at the gray sky and noticed the dark, ominous clouds. She took an unsteady breath and inhaled the scent of rain.

"I can't believe you didn't tell me," Angie said to Cole as they walked to the Starbucks at the corner of her street. She huddled in her jacket to ward off the cool morning breeze but she also wanted to distance herself from Cole. "I never thought you'd lie to me."

"I didn't lie," Cole said calmly. "My parents haven't been part of my life since I was fifteen. They may as well not exist."

"You acted like they were dead. Actually, you let me think they were dead." Angie frowned and shook her head. "Who does that?"

"Angie," he said with a deep sigh. "Don't you think you're overreacting?"

"No," she said as she marched down the crowded sidewalk. She didn't pay attention to the people striding past her or the sound of the bus whooshing by. The world was cold and colorless. Silent and still. She needed to move to get this billowing hurt out of her, but she wasn't getting far.

"It has nothing to do with us," Cole insisted.

Angie stopped and stared at him. "Are you serious?" From the look on his face, he was. How could Cole be so smart and yet so clueless? "It has *everything* to do with us. I always thought you were private. You were reluctant to share anything about yourself, but once you did, I assumed it was the truth. What else have you hidden from me? Is there a Mrs. Cole Foster? Is Cole your real name?"

Cole's eyes narrowed with anger. "Do you really think I would keep something like that from you? What kind of man do you think I am?"

"Are you really thirty years old?" She thought about the other things he had said in the past. Those anecdotes that she had treasured because he had shared them freely. "Did that scar on your arm come from falling out of the tree when you were ten? Are you an only child or do you have a bunch of brothers and sisters I don't know about?"

Cole clenched his jaw and a ruddy streak entered his cheeks. "That's enough," he said in a low growl. "It wasn't easy for me to tell the truth. I knew it wouldn't make me look good but I did it because I *have* been holding back. I was trying to share something and now it just blew up in my face. This is why I don't talk about myself."

"How did you expect I would react?" she asked as she followed him to the Starbucks. "Did you think I would say, 'Oh, thanks for clearing it up, sweetheart. I'm sure that was the only thing you lied about. My trust in you is still absolute.'"

"Wouldn't that have been great?" he muttered as he opened the bright green door and motioned for her to step ahead.

"And why are you telling me now?" She lowered her voice as they entered the long line.

"Like I said, I was trying to share," he bit out the words. "Communicate. Shouldn't I get bonus points for that?"

She rolled her eyes. He just didn't get it. "Don't you think it's too little, too late? We had a booty call and—" The woman standing in front of her turned around and gave a curious look over her thick-rimmed glasses.

Cole lowered his head and whispered, "What we had was more than sex. More than great sex between two people who are still hot for each other."

Angie turned and faced Cole. She saw the desire in his eyes as he remembered.

"It was not a booty call," he whispered in her ear. "It was not a one-night stand. Do I make myself clear?"

"Yes," she answered hoarsely. Last night had meant

something to him, too. He wanted to hold on to their connection. Strengthen it. That was why he was compelled to share something about himself.

She was secretly thrilled but she was still rattled by his revelation. And how long was he willing to share? Until the weekend when the wedding was over? Or was he doing this so they could build something more permanent? Something told her that Cole wouldn't be able to give an answer.

"And I don't want to talk about my parents anymore," Cole said. "They are no longer in my life."

"Are they in jail?" she asked. "Witness protection?"

His expression hardened. "No. The subject is closed."

She took a step closer and touched his forearm. She could tell this was difficult for him, but she needed to know. "Just one more question, I promise."

Cole closed his eyes briefly. "Fine. What is it?"

She wanted to ask why they weren't in his life anymore. Was it his decision or theirs? She couldn't imagine Cole doing something unforgivable.

But he wasn't ready to discuss it. She could see it, sense it. She wanted to know what made him this guarded and cynical.

"Angie?" Angie tensed when she heard Brittany's voice from across the coffeehouse. She saw the redhead from the corner of her eye. "Hey, Angie."

She wasn't going to let Brittany interrupt her. Cole was already regretting telling her. She admitted she hadn't handled this well and she may not get another opportunity. "Were your parents the personal stuff you were dealing with a year ago?"

A muscle bunched in his jaw. "Yes," he said in a hiss. She saw the misery etched in his face. She wished she could soothe him, take the pain away and carry the burden for him. She wanted to protect him from the memories but she didn't know how.

"Angie…" Brittany approached them, her heels clacking loudly on the floor. "Did you get my email about the changes in the wedding ceremony? You haven't responded."

"Sorry. I've been a little busy." She slid her arm around Cole's and gave him an encouraging squeeze. *Lean on me,* she wanted to tell him. *I'll take care of this.* "But, yes, I saw all six emails this morning."

"You know you have to respond to all bridal party emails within an hour of receiving them," Brittany whined. "Those are the rules."

"Along with not getting pregnant, keeping my hair color and no body modifications like tattoos or piercings," Angie added. "Believe me, those rules are burned into my brain."

Brittany crossed her arms and gave Cole a dirty look. "Angie, if I had known you were going to be distracted by a man, I would have also included no dating."

"That's my fault," Cole said, pasting on a polite smile. "When we're together I demand her full attention."

"Well, you need to try and restrain yourself for the weekend. The countdown for my wedding has started and I've already lost one bridesmaid. I can't let anything happen to the rest." Brittany looked at her tiny diamond watch and then at the line. "What is taking so long? My drink is not that difficult to make."

"You couldn't find a replacement for Heidi?" Angie asked.

"Not at this late date," she said with a huff. "It's so

inconvenient. If she had her accident earlier I could have found a substitute."

"You could have Cheryl step in and do it." Cole tilted his head toward her assistant, who was waiting at the counter for their drinks.

"Cheryl?" She gave Cole an incredulous look. "No. She's tiny, blonde and curvy. The other bridesmaids are tall, lean and have black hair. Cheryl would have thrown off the entire color scheme. Anyway, she's my *assistant*."

"Fine, look on the bright side," Angie said, wishing the line would move faster. "Heidi and Robin were not getting along. You would probably have had to deal with a cat fight on your wedding day."

"No kidding." Brittany pressed her hands against her head as if she were getting a headache just thinking about it. "They knew this day had to be perfect but all they cared about was who got to be maid of honor."

"Yeah, I noticed that. So self-involved." And she really didn't understand why they were fighting over what was genuinely becoming a miserable job.

"I should have known they would act this way." She held her hand up as if she were swearing in for office. "I forgot how they were when we were in college. They made my life miserable when I pledged to their sorority. Heidi thought I was on Robin's side and Robin thought I was teaming up with Heidi. Hazing was brutal."

"But you became friends," Cole said with a raised brow.

"Uh, yes. We *are* sorority sisters." She turned to Angie. "Although after my ceremony I'm not going to have them in the same room again."

Angie was recalling what Robin had said at the hospital the other day. The bridesmaid thought she deserved to be the maid of honor. Was it so important to her that she would hurt the competition?

"Nonfat triple-grande sugar-free extra-hot extra-foamy caramel macchiato," the barista called out.

"That's my drink. It's about time," she said as she started to walk away. "Cheryl and I have so much to do and I'm in desperate need of caffeine. Don't forget the mani-pedi at five."

How could she when Brittany sent hourly reminders? "Can't wait."

Cole waited until he saw Brittany and Cheryl exit out the door before he spoke to Angie. "I'm beginning to think Heidi's fall had nothing to do with substance abuse. But I still want to get her blood test results to rule it out."

"I agree." The bespectacled woman in front gave another curious look. Angie beamed a bright smile and tightened her hold on Cole's arm. "We should focus on Robin."

"Robin? No, Brittany."

"Are you kidding?" She looked up at him. "Brittany is trying to make this ceremony perfect. The last thing she wants to do is create problems."

"Didn't you hear what she said? Heidi and Robin were terrible to her when she rushed for a sorority."

"And what better way to get revenge than make them her bridesmaids?" She saw the woman in front of her nod in agreement. "There is a twisted sense of justice in that but Brittany isn't that complex."

"Why do you think it's Robin? She hasn't gotten along with Heidi for years. Why act now?"

"Because Heidi had something Robin wanted."

"And you think she caused an accident so she could

be promoted to maid of honor? No, my money is on Brittany."

"How would she have hurt Heidi?" Angie asked. "She was the center of attention at the bachelorette party."

"Not for the whole party," Cole said. "And who was it that found Heidi? Brittany."

He had a point. "Brittany wouldn't do it," she insisted. At least, she hoped Brittany didn't. The woman was marrying her best friend.

"Maybe we should go back to the strip club and see if it was possible."

Angie groaned. "Do we have to?"

"Don't worry, Angie." He gave a comforting pat on her hand. "I'll be with you every step of the way."

"Okay," she reluctantly agreed. "But first I want you to take me somewhere."

"Name it."

She paused and stared at him. "I want to see your agency."

Cole tilted his head back in surprise. "Why?"

She shrugged. "I'm curious." His apartment and his car never held any personal items. No trinkets, souvenirs or pictures. His office may show something different.

Cole gave a long and deep sigh. "I really am a private investigator."

"I know and I'm sorry I questioned that. I was angry," she said. "You don't have to show me your license. But I've never seen a detective agency and I'm curious."

"It's not that special."

But it may show what was special to him. "Cole, let me be the judge of that."

10

COLE MADE ANOTHER attempt to slide the key into the lock. He hoped Angie didn't see how his hand shook. Quickly glancing at her, he noticed she was brushing her fingers along the lettering on the window.

"Foster Investigations," she read softly. "Sounds very impressive."

He shouldn't be nervous. He was proud of his business. It was small and struggling, however, it was his. The agency was in a neighborhood mostly populated by college students who couldn't afford much and plenty of seniors who'd been there for years. It was humble in every sense of the word, yet he wanted Angie to see what he'd done on his own. He didn't realize how important her opinion was until he opened the door.

He stepped in the outer office and flipped on the lights before he let Angie inside. Glancing around the waiting room, he tried to see it from Angie's perspective. The room was small and beige. There were a few antique chairs, a coffee table and lamps. Nothing that would wow and amaze her.

"This is nice." She trailed her finger along the stained-glass lamp. "I like this. Where did you get it?"

"Antique store," he said gruffly and ignored her look of surprise. He didn't want to explain how he wound up looking at antiques or how he bought the lamp because it had been handed down from generation to generation.

He bought the furnishings more for the story that came along with them. Every piece of furniture he had in his office and in his home had once been important to a family. He didn't have heirlooms of his own, but he took care of the ones people discarded.

Angie stepped in front of a framed print of Norman Rockwell's *The Runaway*. She looked confused and yet charmed as she studied the police officer sitting on a stool at a restaurant while talking to a runaway boy.

When she left the picture and focused on him, he felt as if she were studying something else. She was trying to understand the connection between him and the print. "What kind of clients do you have?" she asked.

It was a simple question and he could give an easy answer, but the knot in his chest tightened. "Families, mostly."

"What do you do for them?"

"Contact missing relatives for one reason or another. I track down people who don't want to be found or think they've been forgotten. A have a few cases finding heirs named in a will and a few deadbeat dads."

Angie strolled around the room. "So the case with Heidi is different for you."

"It's the kind of work I want to do."

She looked at him sharply. "Why is that?"

"Years ago, Heidi and her parents had a falling-out because of her substance abuse. They lost contact with her and they were worried. Heidi didn't know that her family was looking for her. They didn't know if she was alive or in trouble. Now they have a second chance."

"I knew you were good at your job at Missing Persons, but you never explained why it was your passion."

He didn't discuss it because it would have brought up his family life. Working in this field was a constant reminder of what he didn't have. There were no worried parents looking for him. He didn't have a family who wanted him to come home. He had used his skills to find his parents, then waited years to contact them. Unfortunately, they didn't want him to find them.

"What's in here?" she asked as she stood by the doorway that opened into a darkened room.

"That's my office." He almost stopped her from going in. That room felt more personal but there was nothing private in there for her to see. He slowly followed her as she turned on the light. Cole watched her eyes widen when she saw the two mismatched sofas and a low coffee table. A laptop computer sat on a small wooden desk in the far side of the room.

"This isn't at all what I had expected," she said as she slowly entered the room. "I thought I would see a gun collection and a couple of fedoras. It looks like a place where people hang out and talk."

"Most of my work is done on the computer. I use this room when I'm interviewing the families." He spent countless hours listening to people tell their stories, their side. He saw and heard it all. The lies and the excuses. The good and the bad memories. He saw the tears and anger. The shame and the regret.

"I never thought you were a Norman Rockwell fan,"

she said as she pointed at the famous print of a big family having dinner. "You think you know a person…"

He wasn't about to explain the pictures. He didn't think he could. Whenever he looked at them, he felt conflicting emotions. They reminded him of too many broken promises. What he didn't have, but what he could get for others.

Angie sat down on the edge of a sofa. "Okay, I know you're not ready to discuss it, but I have to ask. Were you a runaway? Is that the personal stuff you were going through with your family?"

"Why would you think that?"

"Your interest in missing persons," she said as she began to tick off a list with her fingers. "The pictures in this office. The fact that your family isn't part of your life anymore."

Cole forced himself to remain where he stood. "And you think I chose that?" He couldn't keep the defensiveness out of his voice.

She leaned back on the sofa. "And there's the fact that you walked out on me."

He crossed his arms. "I told you why."

"Yeah, you didn't like the idea of living together. You weren't ready to make a commitment."

"That's not exactly how I would put it."

She glanced at the framed print and then returned her attention on him. "Did you run away from home?"

"No, I stayed." Until he was driven out. Until it was made very clear that his parents did not love him. That no one could love him. "That's when I learned to rely on no one. I had to stand on my own if I wanted to survive."

"That's a very bleak outlook on life."

"It is, but I managed to do that for a long time." He

had survived. Thrived. For a time he had convinced himself that he wasn't missing out. "And then I met you."

She winced and covered her face with her hands. "I scared you off. I knew it."

"Not in the way you think. You made me believe I could be someone different. Someone better. But I can't."

Angie leaned forward and rested her arms on her knees. "Cole, I don't want you to be different."

"You say that now. If we had lived together, you would have kicked me out within a month." Probably sooner, he decided. She would have been under no obligation to stick around.

"Ah."

Cole scowled at her. "I hate when you do that." It meant she had figured out something he rather would have had kept safely hidden.

"That's why you ended our relationship. It wasn't because I was unladylike and too aggressive in bed. It was because I was getting too close."

"Aggressive?" He didn't know if he would call it that.

"You weren't comfortable with me seeing the real you. All of you. Well, guess what, Cole. It wasn't easy for me to bare it all with you."

"Get back to that aggressive-in-bed part."

"Oh, please. What was I supposed to think? We had talked about moving in once and it was maybe a month before you ended things. But two weeks before you left, I had become a little…" She waved her hand as if she were trying to find the right word.

"Demanding?" he said, remembering one intense

night they had shared. "Passionate? Strong? Confident? Take your pick."

"Pushy," she said. "I know guys don't like that much of a challenge in bed and I thought I scared you off."

"Angie, I never had a problem with that. You know what you want and you're not afraid to go after it. That's kind of hot."

"Right," she said with a twist of her lips. "It's so hot that you had to be in charge last night."

"I wanted to show you how much I missed you. How much I still wanted you. I didn't want there to be any question about that." And he had made the wrong move. Instead of showing how he felt, he managed to raise more questions. "Next time you make the first move."

She scoffed at his suggestion but he saw the flare of interest in her eyes. "Like that's going to happen."

"Don't deny it," he said with a knowing smile. He thought of Angie's warmth and affection. "Last night you proved that you want me as much as I want you. You can't keep your hands off me and I don't see why I can't encourage it."

She raised an eyebrow. "What happened to my making the first move?"

He wasn't that patient. He had one night with Angie and he wanted more. He wanted it all. "I never said I was going to be a gentleman about it."

"I should have known," Angie said with a small smile as she rose from the sofa. "In that case, I should leave and remove the temptation."

"Leave?" How could he have gotten this all wrong? "I don't understand."

"I need to meet with Brittany," she said as she headed for the door.

"That's not it. You're making excuses." Cole tried to hide the frustration from his voice. "Why don't you want to make the first move?"

"Because no matter how good we are together, nothing has changed," she said. Angie averted her gaze as she walked away. "History will repeat itself and I can't go through that again."

ANGIE LOOKED AROUND the nail salon Brittany had reserved exclusively for her bridal party. Everything was sleek, modern and blindingly white, from the walls, chairs and tables to the nail technician's uniforms. This was a side of Seattle she didn't know. Located downtown between the famous designer stores and small expensive restaurants, Angie felt on edge.

She wished she were back in Cole's office. She had finally seen a side of him she hadn't expected. He wasn't hiding in that office. If anything, he was sharing with his clients. He was sharing his hopes and his disappointments.

And she couldn't get those framed prints out of her mind. They didn't reflect how she saw Cole—a cynical loner who hid in the shadows. Those pictures represented a positive, almost innocent, time. They obviously meant something to him.

Angie wished she knew more about his life. All this time she had assumed he had been orphaned as a teenager. She had made this conclusion by the few things he said about his childhood and his clear enjoyment of being surrounded by her relatives. She figured he missed having a mother. She assumed he longed for a family. Now she realized that she had been completely wrong about him.

It was a startling feeling. It felt like her world had

shifted. The man she loved was someone else entirely. Or was he? He didn't have contact with his family and the way he acted with her family was genuine. Maybe these clues would give her a better understanding about Cole.

"You look very serious," Robin complained, disrupting her thoughts. "Have another sip of champagne."

"No, thanks." Angie stared at the bright pink polish applied to her toenails. It almost hurt to look at and she was sure it would clash violently against the bile-green bridesmaid dress. "Where have I seen this color?" she asked.

"Definitely not in nature," Robin muttered and shared a smile with her.

Angie snapped her fingers. "Oh, now I remember. It was that drink at the bachelorette party. The psychedelic pink one."

"The Britini," Cheryl said without looking up from tapping the keypad on her phone. "It was made in honor for Brittany's special day."

"I didn't get a chance to try it," Angie said. It didn't sound like her kind of drink, anyway. She didn't drink anything that pink on principle. "What does it taste like?"

"It was a martini made with bubble-gum-infused vodka," Cheryl informed her. "It was a hit at the party."

Angie pursed her lips. "Seriously?"

"They'll have it available during the rehearsal dinner and wedding reception," Cheryl said as she stood up to speak privately on the phone. "You should give it a try."

"Does it really taste like bubble gum?" Angie asked Robin.

"Yes, it's very sweet," Robin confessed in a whisper and looked over to where Brittany was getting her nails done. "But it wasn't a popular drink. Cheryl kept trying to get people to order it because it's named after Brittany."

Heidi probably ordered the drink to please Brittany. She had noticed a bright pink stain when they put Heidi in the recovery position.

"So, how's it going with the stripper?" Robin asked, wagging her eyebrows.

"Stripper?" Oh, right. Cole was supposed to be a stripper. She almost forgot that was how the bridal party met him. She wanted to tell Patrick and her friends what Cole was really doing. That he had been investigating Heidi and needed to know if someone intentionally hurt her. He was determined to find out if it had something to do with her troubled past or if she were in trouble now.

Angie wanted everyone to know that he was using his skills to help others. That he was an honorable and dependable family guy. He was still the man she fell in love with. "His name is Cole. Cole Foster."

"It sounds like it's more than a one-night stand," Brittany called over from where she sat getting her nails done. "I saw them this morning at Starbucks."

"I knew him before the bachelorette party," Angie was quick to clarify. "He's an ex-boyfriend."

Robin leaned back and studied Angie, from her messy ponytail to her tank top and yoga pants. "Yeah, about that. What's his deal?"

Angie frowned. "His deal?"

Robin gestured at her. "Is he into muscular women?"

"Does he have a sports-bra fetish?" Brittany asked with a sly smile.

Angie clenched her jaw. This was why she couldn't

wait for her bridesmaid duties to be over. She could do without the sharp remarks. Just when she thought she was finding common ground with these women, they put her down with a zinger or two. "Is it so strange that he finds me attractive?"

Robin drew back as if she weren't prepared for a pointed question. "Well…no," she said, "but did you get a good look at him? He could have anyone."

"Mmm-hmm," Angie agreed, faking the confidence she wished she had. She leaned back comfortably in her chair. "And if he plays his cards right, he can have me."

"Seriously, Angie—" Brittany took a sip of champagne and gestured to the empty glass "—how did you catch him?"

Angie looked at Brittany and then at Robin. They didn't know anything about Cole. He said little and tried not to show what he was thinking, but the man felt things deeply. Intensely. He tried to keep it in because he felt vulnerable. Unworthy. Cole had been devoted to her but broke up with her because he didn't think he was good enough. What had he said? He was afraid she would have seen his unlovable side.

She knew that feeling. All this time she thought she wasn't good enough for him. That he would eventually dump her for someone glamorous and beautiful. Yet every time he had looked at her, she had felt sexy and brazen. She had seen the desire and adoration in his eyes. She'd seen how his features tightened with lust when she made the first move. She had felt his wonder and awe when they lay exhausted after making love.

But once he was gone, she had questioned everything—the smoldering looks, the secret touches and the anticipation that throbbed between them. They faded from her mind to the point where she thought she'd imagined it all. She'd allowed other people to question and revise what she had shared with Cole. They couldn't understand why he was attracted to her.

"Are you freakishly flexible or something?" Robin asked.

"He's attracted to me because I'm strong, beautiful and smoking hot." At least, that was how he felt when they were dating. She didn't really know if what he felt now was pretend or not.

The women exchanged looks. "Is that what he told you?" Brittany asked with apparent disbelief.

"Yes." Angie smiled and closed her eyes. "Every time he's with me." And during the weekend, she would make sure he found her irresistible.

11

ANGIE TRIPPED WHEN she reached the front door of Foster Investigations. She slapped her hand on the door frame and fought for her balance. Damn shoes. She checked and was grateful no one was around to see how clumsy she was.

How do women walk in these things? She looked down and glared at the black platform heels. Whoever designed them was just evil. Angie stood straight and paused until she stopped wobbling. She smoothed the black bandage dress down her hips and then flipped her long hair over her shoulders.

She was ready. This time she was going to be dressed like the other women at the strip club. Instead of boyish and out-of-place, she would look fun and flirty. Sexy.

She reached for the door and then dropped her hand. What was she trying to do? When Cole saw her, he was going to see this dress as a suggestion. An invitation. Would he see her choice of outfit as the first move?

Angie bit down on her lip and looked back in the direction of the parking lot. It wasn't too late to go home and change. She could always cancel. But deep down, she didn't want to. She wore this dress with Cole in mind. She wanted him to see her as a woman. A sensual and confident woman who didn't let a breakup sideline her.

Angie opened the door and stepped inside the office. "Okay, Cole," she called out from the waiting room. "Let's get this over with."

Cole stepped out of his office. He was rolling down his sleeves and stopped abruptly when he caught a glimpse of her. His eyes widened. "Angie?" he said hoarsely.

She saw the lust in his face. He wasn't even trying to hide it as his gaze traveled leisurely from her eyes to her heels. Her skin tingled with awareness. She felt powerful and exposed at the same time. She wanted to please Cole but she felt like this dress was making a promise she couldn't meet.

Angie suddenly longed for the comfort of her jeans and T-shirts. She wanted to cross her arms and hide the thrust of her breasts. Instead she kept her hands at her sides. "Are you ready?"

Cole slowly walked toward her. His jaw was clenched as his skin flushed. "I don't remember that dress."

"My mom bought it for me last Christmas." It was tradition for her mother to buy a dress and a makeup kit every year. Angie considered it a waste and always felt guilty for not using the gifts but her mother wouldn't let her return them. "I may have to take a picture but I'm worried it would encourage her."

His gaze snagged hers. Her breath caught as she stared into his dark, glittering blue eyes. "You look… wow."

Angie swallowed hard. "Thank you." She felt the tension whipping through him. He wanted her. He wanted to drag her against his body. She could tell he was restraining himself from touching her. Keeping a safe distance, as if he didn't trust himself. "So, what are we looking for? At the strip club?"

"I want to see where Heidi got hurt and decide if it was an accident or a crime. Maybe even come up with a possible weapon," he murmured, distracted by her high hem and bare, toned legs. "Put together a timeline."

"Okay." Angie resisted the urge to tug her dress down. "I still think Robin did it."

He nodded absently and then jerked to a stop as if he remembered something. "I also got Heidi's blood results."

"How did you do that?"

"My clients told me," he said as his gaze lingered on her scooped neckline. "They're taking her back home."

Her breasts felt full and heavy under his gaze. Angie couldn't decide if she wanted to preen or turn away. "That's good, right?"

"It is."

He didn't say anything else. "So what's the problem?" Angie prompted.

He shook his head, as if trying to clear his mind. "She hadn't been drinking," he said, not looking at her. "Apparently she's been sober and clean for years."

"I wonder if Robin or Brittany knew that. I don't think they'd seen her for a while."

"I bet they still view Heidi as a troubled sorority sister," Cole said as he opened the door and gestured for her to go first. "One of them could have tried to make it look like a drunken fall."

"Let's go test our theory." She turned and her heel

snagged on the carpet. Angie reached out and grabbed Cole's arm. His muscle went rigid under her touch. "Sorry."

"Are you going to be okay in those heels?"

"Probably not," she admitted. She held on to his arm. Cole was solid and strong. She felt safe next to him. "I'll just hold on to you, okay?"

"Sure." He reached for her hand and held it against his arm. "I don't mind. Hold on as long as you want."

COLE DIDN'T THINK he would last much longer. The music pulsed a primitive beat. Colorful lights streamed through the dark club. Well-endowed men wearing sequined thongs pranced on the stage and the crowd of women kept screaming for more.

But none of that mattered. All he noticed was Angie. She sat at the bar on a high stool. Her dress had inched up and revealed more of her thighs.

This was a test. He was sure of it.

"What were we thinking?" Cole asked Angie as he stood protectively behind her. He had given every stripper a warning look when they tried to approach. They backed off but he knew it wouldn't last much longer. "This is crazier than the bachelorette party."

Angie swiveled in the chair and her foot bumped against him. "Don't worry, Cole. I'll protect you."

"Very funny," he said as he watched her cross her legs. He was mesmerized by the sensual and fluid motion. His body hardened and his heart pumped harder. Cole gritted his teeth when her skirt drew higher on her thighs.

Angie tilted her head back and smiled. "We'll see how funny it is when these women take one look at you and expect a lap dance."

"They will be disappointed. I dance exclusively for you," he teased. Cole saw her smile dim. "What's wrong?"

"Nothing. Let's consider the timeline. I remember Heidi coming up to us because she wanted a lap dance. She must have gone to the bar after that."

"Why do you say that?"

"She had come over when you were giving me a lap dance." She blushed and looked away. "Heidi had money in her hand but no drink."

"But when we found her there was a drink on the ground next to her."

"It was a Britini. I'm told it's the drink of the wedding. Would Heidi have ordered one to please Brittany?"

"If so, she would want Brittany to see it." He looked around the room. "Brittany wasn't on stage the whole time. The attention was on the dancers. It would have been easy for Brittany to lose herself in the crowd."

"She wore a tiara and a bright red dress. Brittany would have been noticed," Angie said. "And why do you think it was Brittany? It doesn't make sense."

"They could have had a fight," Cole said. "Or Brittany could have seen an opportunity and jumped on it."

"Robin was the one who really hated Heidi. She didn't try to hide it."

"But it sounds like the wedding preparations brought forward a lot of hurtful memories. Remember, Heidi and Robin had been her tormentors when she first rushed the sorority." He looked around the club. "There was nothing here that could be used as a weapon. Unless Brittany brought it and left with it."

"No," Angie said as she reached for her drink. "Security checks the purses."

"Wait a second…" He looked at the tables near the stage. There was nothing on the tabletops except for purses and drink glasses. "The flowers."

"There are no flowers," she said against the rim of her glass.

"Exactly. There were flowers at the bachelorette party."

"Oh, yeah." Angie rolled her eyes. "Brittany wanted the same flowers that would be at the wedding. You would not believe how expensive that turned out to be. It took forever to find the vases that she wanted."

"Were they heavy?"

"They were metallic." She paused and then raised her eyebrows. "Oh, I see what you're saying. Yes, they were heavy enough to cause injury."

"Where are they now?"

Angie shrugged. "Cheryl will know. She has a checklist for everything."

"Whoever did this had nerves of steel. Somehow she hit Heidi and then had the presence of mind to put the flowers back, leaving the scene undisturbed."

"You still have to find the vase." Angie saluted him with her drink. "Good luck with that."

Cole saw a glimmer of sequins from the corner of his eye. He turned and saw Tiger, the most popular stripper in the club, walking toward them. Cole saw the appreciative look Tiger had for Angie. Cole grabbed her hand. "Let's get out of here."

"Wait." Angie clumsily set down her glass. "I wasn't finished."

"Hey, lady." Tiger stood in front of Angie and flexed his chest muscles. "How about a lap dance?"

Angie stared at him. "Who, me?"

"That's not going to happen." Cole had to fight back

the raw, ugly emotions that poured through him. He felt possessive. Territorial. He helped Angie out of her chair and dragged her away. "No one gives this woman a lap dance but me."

"Cole? What is your problem?" Angie asked as she hurried behind him as fast as her heels would allow. "I could have taken care of that myself."

"I declined for you. You're welcome." And yet he wondered if Angie would have accepted the dance out of curiosity or attraction. His gut twisted at the thought.

She tugged hard at his hand as they exited the building. The cold rain pelted them and they huddled together. "Cole, listen to me."

"Once we're in the car." He tried to shelter her as he guided her to the parking lot. Their shoes splashed in the puddles and Angie slipped. He put his arms around her, holding her securely against him until he got her safely in the car.

"You don't speak for me," she said the moment he slid into the driver's seat. "And you don't have any claim on me."

"Yes, I do." He wouldn't let her deny that.

"Because of last night?" she asked as she brushed her damp hair from her face. "That doesn't mean we're back on."

Cole rested his hands on the steering wheel. What would it take to get her back in his life? How many tests would he have to pass to make up for what he'd done? There were some things he knew he wouldn't accept.

"Did you want the guy to dance for you?" he asked accusingly. The idea sickened him. "Did you want me to watch? Give you dollar bills so you could have every stripper in there?"

Her mouth dropped open. "No! I don't want any of those guys. I—"

"Good." He reached for Angie and kissed her. Threading his fingers in her hair, he held the base of her head as he deepened the kiss. He needed to claim her. Brand her with his kiss. It was only fair—he was hers and always has been.

Cole felt the soar of triumph when she softened against him. But then she went stiff and pulled away. Angie drew back in her seat. Her chest rose and fell as she glared at him. "What was that for?"

"Come on, Angie." He didn't mean for his voice to sound harsh, but he was fighting a desperation he didn't understand. He wanted Angie, but he wanted Angie to accept him, as well. "You want this as much as I do. It's been a long time for both of us."

"And you think I would be an easy tumble in bed?" she asked, her voice rising with anger. "Because the guys told you I don't date? That I haven't looked at another guy since you left?"

"I wasn't thinking that at all." But it had given him hope. He wanted it to be a sign that he could fix the mess he'd made. That they shared a bond that couldn't be broken.

"What are you thinking?"

He shoved his hand in his hair. "That I want to drag you into the backseat, rip off that insanely sexy dress and—"

"So you want me."

"Yes."

Angie didn't look away. "Right now."

"Yeah." Immediately, if not sooner. He was rock-hard and had been the moment he saw her in that dress. There would be no foreplay and no lingering touches.

It would be a hard and fast ride the moment he sank into her.

"And then what?" she asked. "What about tomorrow or the next day? How long do you plan to hang around until you walk away again?"

Cole stared at her. Didn't she see that he was still crazy for her? That he wanted to try again. He wasn't planning to walk away again. It nearly broke him the last time. He didn't have the strength to do it again. "I'm here to stay."

Angie crossed her arms. "Why?"

"It's very simple." He pointed at her. "I want you." He pointed at himself. "You want me."

Her mouth formed in a disbelieving smile. "That wasn't enough before."

He scoffed at that statement. "I've always wanted you. From the moment I met you." He had seen her in the gym and had been immediately thunderstruck. He had tried to impress her with his strength and speed only to discover she was just as strong and fast as he was. If she thought that would scare him off, it had the opposite effect. He had been more intrigued than ever.

"But you went away and you stayed away," she pointed out. "You didn't contact me until you needed help on this case. Then you had to pretend to be hot for me. How do you think that makes me feel?"

"I have no idea what's going through your mind. You are driving me crazy. What do you want from me?"

"I want the truth," she said. "The whole truth."

He looked into her eyes. "You are everything I want in a woman."

She blinked, obviously not expecting to hear those words. "What do you want from me now?" she asked.

"Forgiveness? Sex? Do you want to be friends with benefits?"

He held her gaze as the fear pulsed through him. It was too soon to say anything but he had to take the risk. "I want another chance."

She lowered her gaze. "I don't think I can do that again," she whispered.

He held on to the steering wheel and squeezed as the pain rushed through him. "Because I made one mistake."

"No, because I can't be with a guy who won't share his life."

"I just did this morning," he blurted out in frustration. He shared something about his past and it did not go well. "Look at what happened."

"That was one time and you're still holding back," she accused. "You don't trust me. Not enough."

"That's not true," he insisted. "I trust you more than anyone I know."

"You don't trust me enough to talk about yourself. I don't know about your past, I didn't know about your dream of opening an agency and I don't know how you feel about me. And I was with you for over a year." She took a deep breath. "Cole, I'm done with this. This was a mistake."

Cole closed his eyes as her words ripped through him. He was not a mistake. "Angie…"

"Just take me back to your office. I parked my car there," Angie said. Her voice was dull and tired as she looked out the car window. "We got caught up in the pretense. Let's forget this ever happened."

12

As COLE PARKED in the front of his office building, he felt the weight of this moment. He knew he had to do something or Angie would never be his again. Angie, the only woman he loved and if he were honest, still loved.

Angie had been the most loyal person he knew. She didn't agree with everything he did, but she was there for him. She cheered him on when he needed encouragement and gave him advice when he asked. When he made a mistake, she called him on it. This was a woman he wanted at his side. Yet he never thought she would reach the point where she called it off. But he had found her limit.

That was his specialty. Driving people away.

"We need to talk," he said as he put the car in Park.

"Cole, I'm done talking."

"It won't take long," he said as he watched her unbuckle her seat belt. "Just come into my office. There are a couple of things I need to tell you."

"Like what? About your case?" She exhaled sharply. "Face it, Cole. The whole thing was probably an accident. I can see how it happened after wearing these stupid heels all night. Heidi likely spilled her drink and fell. She hit her head. I don't know why she was facedown. She could have tried to get up but failed."

"That makes sense." His instincts told him something different, but he had no proof. It was time to stop and move on to the next assignment.

"Your case is over," she continued. "Heidi's family reconnected with her. You don't have to investigate anymore. You don't have to go to the rehearsal dinner or the wedding. It's all good."

There was something about Angie's voice that bothered him. She sounded tired. Disappointed. She sounded like she was giving up on him. "That's not what I want to talk about," he said, his voice rough as the fear clawed his chest. "Come on, let's go inside."

Angie paused before she gave a sigh of defeat. "Fine. But you have five minutes."

He helped her out of the car. The rain was now a mist, clinging to their skin and clothes. Angie didn't touch him or hold on to his arm as she navigated the puddles. She didn't say a word as they walked into his office suite. She didn't look around but headed straight for the other room, slapping the light switch as she entered.

"Well?" Angie asked once he stepped into the room after her. "What is so important that we had to discuss it here?"

He took a deep breath but it didn't diminish the nervous energy coursing through his veins. "You're right," he said as he started to pace. "I didn't trust you enough. I didn't realize it until you said it just now."

Angie didn't say anything. She stood by the sofa, arms crossed, as she watched him walk around the small room. She glanced at her wristwatch and the fear gripped him harder. He needed to explain himself and reveal his darkest moments, but he didn't think he could do that under the clock.

"I didn't tell you some things about me because..." He floundered, trying to come up with the right words. He wasn't much of a talker and what he said now would have a great impact on his future. "Because it would open some old wounds."

"It was more than omitting a few important facts," she pointed out. "You lied to me. You led me to believe that you didn't have a family. Why would you lie about something like that?"

"I felt..." He stopped and gathered all the courage he had. "I felt that if you knew all about me, saw the real me, you would leave."

"Okay, that's kind of what you said before. I'm not really sure where this is heading." She sat down on the sofa. "Is there something you've done in your past that I should know about?"

"No." He crossed his arms tightly. "It's about the personal stuff I was going through when we were together. You suggested moving in and that—"

"Scared you off, I know." She leaned back into the sofa and crossed her legs. "You didn't want to make that kind of commitment."

"No, you're wrong. I *wanted* to make a commitment." When she had made the suggestion, he wanted to instantly agree before she would have changed her mind. "But I didn't want to make the mistakes I'd made in the past."

He saw the hurt and surprise flash in her eyes. She pressed her lips together. "You lived with someone before me?"

"No, I didn't want to before. I'm not easy to live with. I never have been." He made a face. That was an understatement. He had chosen not to live with anyone, not even a roommate when he was younger, because he knew they would grow to resent and hate him. He hadn't been interested in living with a girlfriend until he met Angie.

She made him want things he told himself he couldn't have. She showed him a world that sounded almost too good to be true. He knew it wouldn't last. He would ruin it just like he always did.

"I wanted…" He paused and tried again. "I wanted to know where I went wrong before I moved in with you. In the past, I had pushed away the people I love. Like my parents."

Angie frowned. "So, what did you do?"

"I tracked them down." It had been incredibly easy. They weren't trying to hide. Not from the government or the rest of the world. Their goal was simple: they wanted to be rid of him.

"Your parents?" She glanced at the family dinner picture on his wall and then back at him. "How long had it been since you'd seen them?"

"Fifteen years." He looked at the floor as he remembered that horrible day. He usually tried not to think about it, or relive that sense of absolute rejection and fear. "One day I had returned home from school and they were gone."

She blinked and leaned forward. "I'm sorry, what?"

"My mom and my stepdad had left me." He rubbed the back of his neck as he felt the heat flood his skin. "There was no note or any contact information. They had taken all their stuff and took off while I was at school."

Her eyes narrowed. "I don't understand."

"I wasn't a runaway, Angie," he said gruffly as he felt the dark emotions welling up inside him. "I was a throwaway. They kicked me out of the family because they didn't want me. They left and started another life."

She stared at him. "What did you do? How did you survive?"

"My friends helped me a lot. But there were nights when I had to live on the streets. I kept going to school because it was warm and I could get a meal. It took a while before I got enough jobs and could support myself."

"Why would your parents leave?"

"My stepfather and I always fought. He was bigger than me and would hit me often. One day he hit me and I hit back hard." His mouth twisted as he remembered how powerful he had felt. He had believed that his stepfather couldn't hurt him anymore. How wrong he had been. "The next day my parents were gone."

"It's taken you this long to track your mom?"

"No." He went and sat next to Angie on the sofa. He felt weary and old. Thinking about that time in his life always dragged him down. "I found out her information a long time ago but I didn't go searching for them. And they definitely weren't interested in looking for me."

"They told you that?" she asked, clearly horrified.

"They didn't have to." He saw it in their faces when he found them. They asked no questions about him or his life. They just wanted him gone. "But when you talked about moving in, I knew I had to find them and answer some questions."

"Did they give you any answers?"

"No." He regretted looking for his mom and step-father.

Angie was quiet for a few minutes before asking, "Where do they live?"

"Across the country. Virginia." He shifted as the image of his mom's new home bloomed in his mind. It was tiny but well-loved. It was a house he would have been grateful to grow up in. "They're doing better than when I lived with them."

"I can't believe your parents didn't look after you." Angie curled in closer. She wrapped her arm around his chest. "They messed up. Not you. What mother would do that?"

"My mother never wanted me. I was an accident." She had ranted about it so many times. How his biological father abandoned them when she got pregnant. How no man wanted her because he was part of the package. How he had better not mess it up with his stepfather. "I was a mistake that changed the course of her life."

"You're not a mistake." Angie leaned her head against his shoulder. "When your parents left you to fend for yourself? That's a mistake. That's a crime."

"I survived." Barely. There were times when he wanted to give up, but pride kept him going. He had been determined to show his parents that he could take care of himself. He had carried the fantasy that his parents would eventually come crawling back to him begging for forgiveness.

"Why didn't you tell me when you found them?" Angie asked. "You didn't need to keep it a secret."

"All this time I thought they were incapable of loving anyone. But I was wrong. They were incapable of loving me. There was something wrong with me."

She pressed her hand against his chest. "That's not true. Don't ever think that."

"It is true. I know because when I tracked them down, my mother was still married to my stepfather. They were happy and doing well." The pain tightened his throat and it hurt to tell the rest of the story. "And they had more children."

She lifted her head. "No."

"Two girls, not yet teenagers." It had been a jarring discovery when he met his half sisters. He had been devastated. "My mom and stepfather take good care of them and are very involved parents."

And if their desertion had been the wound, seeing his parents transform into good parents had been the twist of the knife. It was as if they wanted to start from scratch instead of a do-over. They were able to give those girls a secure and stable home life. Why couldn't they have done it for him when he needed it the most?

"Oh, my God." Angie's eyes held of sheen of tears. "What did your mom say when you found her? Was she ashamed of what she did?"

"No." By the time he had realized that, he had been numb. "She had to make a decision between my stepfather and me. She picked him and she doesn't regret it. And she made it very clear that she doesn't want anything to do with me."

Angie didn't know how long she sat with Cole as they held each other. She wished she could do something to take the pain away. She wanted him to know that he was loved, but she knew he wouldn't believe her.

She gave him a light punch on his shoulder. "You should have told me."

He reached up and covered his hand over hers. "It's

difficult to talk about it. My friends' parents would let me stay for a while but they were suspicious. People looked at me differently when they learned the truth. They wanted to know what horrible thing I did to cause my parents to leave. I was a lot of trouble. I wasn't an easy child to love."

"Are you kidding me? You're still taking the blame for what they did?" What kind of mind games did they play on Cole? The anger boiled inside her. "You should have taken me with you. We had been partners. We were in this together."

He squeezed her hands. "I didn't know what I was going to face."

"So you went alone to protect me?" That shouldn't surprise her. He made decisions, dealt with problems and took actions by himself. "Don't do that again."

"Again?" he asked in a teasing tone. "I thought you were done with me."

"Stop throwing my words back at me," she said in a grumble. "I can't believe they left you alone to fend for yourself. That is not acceptable. It's a good thing I didn't meet them or I would have kicked their asses." She glared at Cole when he smiled. "What? This isn't a laughing matter."

"I love seeing this side of you. It's sweet."

"Sweet?" She didn't feel sweet. She was enraged and there was nothing she could do about it. She couldn't shield Cole from the hurt his family had caused him. "You should have told me."

"It's not easy to share. I was ashamed. I still feel like there's something wrong with me. Something…"

Unloveable. She pressed a kiss on his cheek. "You shouldn't be."

He looked away. "You don't know my mom's side of this."

She cupped his face and looked into his eyes. "It doesn't matter. I know who you are. I know what kind of man you've become. I will always be on your side." She touched her lips to his. "Thank you for telling me. It explains a couple of things."

Cole winced. "Like what?"

"Your interest in finding missing persons, the pictures in this office." His inability to commit, she added silently. He wanted to, but there was no way he would overcome his family's desertion.

"I don't like the sound of that," Cole said.

Angie realized that he was feeling exposed. He was a loner who felt more comfortable in the shadows. She awkwardly patted his shoulder and moved to get up. "I should go now."

"Stay." The one word sounded more like a plea than a command. His hands were still on her back but she could easily leave.

She wanted to stay. She loved him—always had, always would—but it wasn't right. She should get up and go before she got too attached again.

"Please," he whispered as he brushed his mouth against hers.

She'd stay, Angie decided as she leaned into him and kissed him. She wanted him for one night. She wanted everything and was willing to take the risk. Starting now.

As she kissed him softly, Angie felt an overwhelming need to touch him. Caress his chest and hug him. Hold his hand and take away his pain. She wanted to protect him and show him love. But a part of her knew that kind of slow intimacy would scare off Cole.

Her lips clung to his before Cole pulled way. She wasn't sure what she'd expected when he opened his eyes. His vulnerability tore at her. She knew he was wary of her. He was unsure of what her kiss meant.

She kissed him again, pouring everything she felt into it. She wanted to tell him how much she loved him. That she wanted to be with him, share the good and the bad. But he wasn't ready to hear that. He may never be.

Cole moaned and broke off the kiss. "Wait a second," he said as he held her an arm's length away. "Just a few minutes ago you thought this was a mistake. That *I* was a mistake."

Angie pulled at the front of his shirt and drew him closer. "I was wrong." She never should have used the word *mistake*. It brought up bad memories and deep insecurities.

"All of a sudden you're wrong?" he asked as he lowered her down on the sofa and lay on top of her.

"Because now I understand," she said as she tilted her hips, cradling Cole against her. She understood what drove him away. Now she knew he had been betrayed by his loved ones.

She also knew he was very private, but now she had a reason why he felt safer alone. She wanted him to know that not only was he safe with her, but she would also protect him and give him strength by being at his side.

Cole slid his hand over her bare leg and pulled off her shoe. He tossed it across the room and the other shoe followed. Angie wrapped her legs tightly around his waist. She held him close as she trailed a string of hard, fast kisses along his throat. She smiled when she felt the rumble of a growl against her mouth.

Cole hiked her skirt up and placed his hand between

her legs. He stilled. "Are you completely naked under this dress?" he asked hoarsely.

"Yes," she said. His touch felt incredible. She wanted more.

"It's a good thing I didn't know that until now. I wouldn't have been able to concentrate before." He stroked her and Angie shivered with delight.

She moaned as the anticipation built. Cole always knew just how to tease her, dipping his finger into her wet heat before withdrawing completely. And doing it over and over until she writhed underneath him. "Please, Cole."

He didn't follow her request. Instead, Cole slipped off the sofa and placed her feet on the floor. For a moment Angie thought he was ending this before it started. She reached out for him just as he kneeled between her legs. Her stomach tightened with excitement as he splayed her legs and placed his mouth on her sex.

Angie bucked her hips at the first flip of his tongue. She gripped the back of his head, her fingers winding through his hair, as he pleasured her. She wanted to hold on to this moment, but this night was supposed to be for him. She meant to show him love but got caught up in the sensations that only Cole could provide.

"You shouldn't," she murmured as she gently lifted her hips. Angie gasped when his tongue touched her clit.

"I want to," he said against her skin. "Let me."

She reluctantly let go of his hair. Angie gave a keening cry as he explored her with his mouth and fingertips. The hot need pulled deep in her pelvis, growing stronger.

Her climax came suddenly, pulsing hard through her body. It stole her breath as her skin went hot. Angie tightened her legs against Cole as she clutched his head. She rode out the wicked pleasure before sagging against the sofa.

She was aware of Cole taking off her clothes. She was limp and spent, her mind buzzing, as Cole tugged the snug outfit off of her. Her small breasts swung freely as he discarded the dress. She reached for him, their fingers colliding as they pulled at his shirt.

Their uneven breaths and the rustle of clothing were the only sounds in the room. The rush of blood pounded in her ears as Cole stood before her naked. She slowly licked her lips as she stared.

He was magnificently masculine, from his broad shoulders and wide chest to his powerful thighs and thick penis. Angie's core clenched as she noticed his arousal. His skin was flushed and his muscles were trembling with barely leashed restraint. Cole was ready to pounce.

He reached for her, his hands firm but urgent, and he laid her down on the floor. She felt the crumpled dress and the soft carpet underneath her spine. Cole was on his knees in front of her, his hands caressing her breasts, resting at her hips. She felt the nervous flutter of excitement as he surged into her.

"Hold on to me," he said roughly.

She pressed her body against him, acutely aware of their differences. His hard chest ground into her soft breasts. His movements were rushed and urgent while her hands lingered on his heated skin. She moved beneath him, yielding to his demanding thrusts.

Angie curled her arms and legs around Cole. She burrowed her head into his neck as he drove into her. She felt his desperation. The wildness poured through him. Cole let out a hoarse cry as he pulsed in her. He thrust one last time before he sank onto her.

Angie welcomed his weight and his heat. She welcomed him back into her heart. And this time, she wouldn't let him go.

13

Angie woke up with a start. She looked around, her heart pounding. The room was shadowy and quiet. It took her a second to realize that she was in Cole's office. She was on the sofa with a soft fleece tucked around her.

She noticed her dress was lying still crumpled on the floor next to her heels. Cole's clothes were gone. "Cole?" she called out. She waited but there was no response.

Slowly sitting up, Angie glanced at the windows. The shades were pulled down but she could tell by the shadows that it was wet and gloomy outside. She looked at the clock in the office and saw that it was early morning.

Where was Cole? She glanced at the closed door. It felt wrong waking up alone. She was used to rising in the early morning with him. They took their time getting out of bed, unwilling to break apart.

Don't think about that. That is in the past, Angie reminded herself. And she wouldn't read in to Cole's absence, either. It wasn't a big deal.

She wiggled into the bandage dress. Great, she thought as she combed her hair with her fingers. She stayed out all night the one time she wears a dress and heels. Now she gets to do the walk of shame.

I've done nothing to be ashamed about, Angie thought as she scooped up her shoes. She made love to Cole because she wanted to. She loved him and she wanted to be with him. Last night she felt closer to him than ever before.

Damn. She was still in love with him. She had been prepared to break it off because he wouldn't let her get close. But last night gave her hope. He opened up and trusted her with his most painful secret.

Angie looked at the framed print of the family dinner and shook her head. She couldn't imagine what Cole went through. She wanted to take that pain away and carry it for him. But the only thing she could do was offer him understanding and patience.

She wasn't sure what her next move should be. Angie suspected that Cole would feel awkward with her. He'd revealed something he clearly wasn't comfortable sharing. Nothing she said to him would make him believe he wasn't responsible for his parents' desertion. He'd left her a year ago because he thought it had only been a matter of time before she was going to leave him.

And she almost did last night. He knew it, too. Otherwise he wouldn't have told her about his past. She knew she had to show him that she wasn't going to leave. Not now, not when she finally understood why he was so private and why he kept pushing her away. He was waiting for her to see him as too much trouble and break up with him.

She strode into the waiting room barefoot just as

she heard the key in the lock. Angie's heart leaped and she smiled when Cole entered the office carrying two cups of coffee.

He skidded to a stop. "You're up."

"Morning." She couldn't contain the joy inside her. She felt gloriously, vibrantly alive. She took a step forward, ready to open her arms wide and greet him with a loving embrace and a long kiss.

"Here, this is for you." He held out a coffee cup.

"Oh…" She stopped in midstep and slowly dropped her arms. Her chest tightened as she saw the hunted look in his eyes. He didn't want to be here. Correction, she thought, as the joy fizzled, he didn't want to be here with her. "Thanks."

She was the one who felt awkward as she accepted the cup. She noticed how careful Cole was not to let their hands touch. She glanced up through her lashes but he wasn't looking at her.

"Are you okay?" she asked quietly.

"Me? Yeah." He held his coffee cup with both hands. "You?"

She knew he was ready to bolt. Whatever she did next was important. She had to tread carefully.

Angie stared at the cup as she turned it in her hands. "About the wedding rehearsal tonight…"

"I'm going." His voice was harsh.

How did he know what she was going to say? "You don't have to."

"We made a deal," he reminded her. "I'll keep my side of the bargain."

"But that was when you needed to look into Heidi's accident," she said. "The whole reason we pretended to be together was so you could get behind-the-scenes access. That's no longer an issue."

He gave her a cold look, his eyes narrowed and his jaw set. Cole suddenly moved and set his coffee on the table. "Angie, do you want me to stay away from the wedding?"

"What? No!" She was making a mess out of this.

"You were ready to get rid of me last night. You're still trying. But I gave my word and I'm taking you to the rehearsal dinner and the wedding."

"I wasn't trying to get rid of you." She closed her eyes. "I thought we were getting caught up in the pretense."

Cole looked at the floor and shuffled his feet. She saw the tips of his ears turn bright red. "I know that last night was…"

Awesome. Amazing. Incredible. Take your pick. She held her breath as she waited for Cole's next words.

He exhaled and started again. "Last night you gave me comfort when I needed it."

She blinked as he said those words in a rush. "Comfort?" she repeated. "You think that was comfort?" She gave him her heart and soul. She showed him how she felt with every touch and every kiss.

"You're important to me, Angie," he continued. "Though last night I didn't know if I was out of your life or back in your bed. You obviously don't know what you want but I don't want to be pushed out and then pulled back in over and over. I've had enough of that in my life and I don't need it from you. We've finally got back to where we are friends and I don't want to risk that over last night."

She flinched as his words drove into her like a twisted knife. *Friends?* They just made love and he wanted to be *friends?* Angie swiped the tip of her tongue along her dry lips. "Do you usually have sex with your friends?"

"I've never had a friend who was a woman," he admitted. "It's different with you. I think this is all I can handle right now."

That hurt. She loved him and he didn't love her like that. He didn't love her enough. She was in the same place she was a year ago. Only this time, she thought they were getting closer. Instead, she pushed him too hard, too soon. This guy didn't want a second chance anymore. She'd scared him off. The best he could offer was friendship.

"So…" He gave her a quick look. "We're good?"

She wanted to hide. She had put herself out there and had given him everything. She was renewing her commitment to Cole but he wanted to keep her at a distance. It was like a slap in the face but she refused to show her hurt.

"Sure," she said, praying that he couldn't see she was dying inside. "You never can have enough friends."

14

"THAT WAS THE longest wedding rehearsal ever," Angie muttered to Cole. They were standing at the window of the fancy restaurant in Seattle's downtown waterfront district and watching the other guests at the post-rehearsal dinner. She was glad he was there with her. She could express her real feelings with him. "I am starving. I don't think I can face another of Brittany's home videos without something in my stomach."

"That rehearsal was pretty intense," Cole said. "I'm not surprised Robin kept making mistakes. Brittany was putting a lot of pressure on her."

Angie rubbed her stomach and looked longingly at the empty table settings. "I don't know who was the worst taskmaster, the bride or the minister."

"Cheryl," Cole decided. He had sat quietly in the back of the church, thinking it would be a quick walkthrough of the ceremony. An hour later he had been stunned at the focus on detail. "She is like a drill sergeant."

"How can someone that tiny be so scary?" Angie

leaned against the wall and studied Brittany's assistant. "I think the best man may be traumatized for life."

Cole looked at where Cheryl stood. At first glance the curvy blonde appeared almost sweet and nonthreatening. Maybe it was the pink leopard-print dress or the way she flirted with the men. But Cheryl was tenacious and didn't back down until she got the results she wanted.

He cast a quick glance at Angie, who wore a black pantsuit and flat shoes. The jacket was big and her shirt was buttoned all the way to the high collar. The pants had a wide leg. Last night she wore a skintight dress that showed a lot of skin. Tonight she was hiding her body. Her femininity. She was dressed similar to the groomsmen.

"What's with the suit?" he asked.

She slowly looked at him and then at her outfit. "What's wrong with it?" she asked with warning.

He shrugged. "I liked what you wore last night." The little black dress had been out of her comfort zone. She had shown a side of herself she wasn't confident about. But she had given him a glimpse and he thought it meant something.

"You made that obvious," she said. "But don't read anything into it. It wasn't like I was dressing for a date. I wore it so I would blend in at the strip club."

"And what is this?" He reached out and flipped the lapel. The fabric was surprisingly soft.

She straightened the jacket lapel. "This is what I wear when I'm hanging out with the guys." Angie glared at him. "Why the sudden interest in my outfit?"

"Why the sudden interest in hiding behind several layers of clothes?" he countered. "You weren't last night."

"I'm not hiding. You are," she accused. "We made love last night and then you turn around and say 'Hey, thanks for comforting me. Let's stay friends. No hard feelings.'"

Made love? Her choice of words intrigued him. "I was doing you a favor. My past is my burden, not yours. I knew you would see me differently and I was giving you an out."

"You weren't giving me a choice. You're pushing me away. *Again,*" Angie stressed. "Only this time you're not walking away. No, this time you're putting me in the friend zone where you know I don't want to be."

"How am I supposed to act? You were the one calling it quits last night. I tried to do better. And suddenly we're having sex because you felt sorry for me. Excuse me if I don't jump up and down with joy for getting pity sex from you."

"Pity sex?" she hissed, her eyes wide. "Cole, that wasn't pity. That was…"

"What?" he asked when she stopped and pressed her lips together. "See? This is what I get when I tell you stuff. I don't want your pity. I'm not a charity case. I'd rather have your anger than have you feel sorry for me."

"That's not how I see you," she said. "I see a man who struggled and made something of himself without the support of a family. I see a guy who tracks down the forgotten because he had once been left behind. That's not pity, Cole."

Cole stared in her eyes. She was sincere, but there was something else. Respect? Love? He couldn't be sure. His heart started to pound. "Then what—"

"Angie," Robin said as she approached them. Her cloud of perfume enveloped them when she stopped at Angie's side. She gave them both a cautious look. "Am I interrupting something?"

Angie was the first to break eye contact. "No, Robin. Not at all," she said with a polite smile. "What's up?"

How could she do that? Cole wondered. She had him off balance and desperate for answers. He wanted to drag Angie away from this party and find out if he still had a chance with her. Instead, he clenched his hands and tried to find the last of his patience.

"Did you notice that you're in every picture and video with Patrick?" Robin asked, gesturing at the television screen set up in the corner, causing her martini to slosh in the glass. "I didn't realize you two were that close."

"They've been best friends since kindergarten," Cole said. Friendships were important to Angie. Her circle of friends was small but long-lasting. She'd break up with a boyfriend but her friends were forever.

"And you never went on a date?" Robin asked as she took a sip of her drink. "Not even once?"

"What can I say?" Angie said with a shrug. "I'm always in the friend zone."

Cole stiffened. He knew that was aimed at him. "That's not true," he said as he grasped the end of her ponytail. "Becoming your basketball buddy was the last thing on my mind when I met you."

"That's because I'm better at basketball," Angie said before she turned away and faced Robin. "I've never dated those guys but they've given me lots of dating advice."

"And none of their tips worked," Cole pointed out as he gave her hair a tug, demanding her attention. Her friends had tried to make her into the kind of woman they'd date. He had wanted the real Angie. A woman who could challenge him on the field and who could bring him to his knees with a simple touch.

"Weird." Robin smacked her lips and frowned at her martini glass. "Have you tried the Britini? It's really sweet but it has a kick."

"No, thanks." Angie held her hand up as Robin offered the glass.

"It tastes a little different tonight. I'm not sure why." Robin puckered her lips. "So, tell me, Angie. Which of the groomsmen are single?"

Angie jerked her head back at the maid of honor's question. "Tim and Steven. I don't think either of them even brought dates tonight."

"Good." Robin leaned against the wall and studied the men on the other side of the room. "I haven't decided which one I want."

"For what?" Angie asked.

"A bridesmaid always hooks up at a wedding." Robin gave her a strange look. "How do you not know this?"

Angie turned to Cole. "I haven't heard of that tradition."

"It doesn't apply to you because I'm your date," he said as he wrapped his finger around her ponytail. "Don't forget it."

"How could I?" Angie said sweetly.

"Angie, you hit the jackpot and landed a stripper. It really isn't fair." Robin rubbed her forehead and looked at her martini glass. "I probably should put this down. It's stronger than I remember and it's giving me a headache."

Angie tried to step away from his hold but he wasn't letting go. He was rewarded with a glare as Robin set down her glass at her assigned seat.

"So, you know all the guys here, right?" Robin asked Angie as she tugged her pink strapless dress in place. "Which ones have you dated?"

"None of them," Angie replied.

"Seriously?" Robin studied the men and then studied Angie. "Not one of these guys made a move on you? What are you doing wrong?"

The question seemed to fluster Angie. "I…I don't…"

Cole curled his arm around her waist. "The problem with growing up with these guys," he said, "is that there's no mystery left. They know each other's secrets, embarrassing moments and questionable dating history."

"Ah, got it. Finding out is half the fun." Robin fluffed out her hair and yanked up her strapless dress. "I'm going to go flirt with the redhead. What's his name? Tim? Wish me luck."

"Let go of my hair," Angie told Cole as she watched Robin sashay toward the group of men. "Don't make me pull out my self-defense moves."

"You should know better than to put your hair in a ponytail. It puts you at a disadvantage." Cole said as he reluctantly let go.

She felt like Cole was the one who put her at a disadvantage. She was very aware of him and she couldn't think straight. Her skin tingled when he touched her and she wanted to lean into him when he drew near. But he didn't seem to have the same problem. He wanted to just be friends.

"I have to ask since Robin brought it up," Cole said. "Why haven't you dated any of those guys?"

"There was no mystery left," she said in a monotone. "We know each other's secret—"

He stepped closer and rested his hand on her hip. "The real reason," he whispered in her ear.

They're not you. Cole was a mix of strength and gentleness, of hard-earned wisdom and quiet humor. She was amazed at his level of curiosity and patience. He was everything she wanted in a man. In a partner. No man could compare to Cole.

Maybe that was why she was thinking of marriage when they hadn't discussed it. She saw something in Cole that he didn't see in himself. He didn't have a family but he valued the connection so much that he dedicated his life's work to reuniting relatives. When they had been together, she instinctively knew he had claimed her as his own. His way of making a commitment wasn't by living together or exchanging vows. He would protect and take care of her, even if it meant keeping his distance.

"Come on, Angie," he cajoled. "You can tell me the truth. Why haven't you dated any of the men in your life?"

"Lack of interest," she finally said. "On my part and on theirs."

"Don't be too sure about that." He gave a sidelong look at her friends. "I think Tim has always had a crush on you."

She rolled her eyes. "You weren't worried about that while we were dating. But why should you? You knew no one would notice me."

"That's because you don't want to be noticed," he accused. "It's like you want to be invisible. The day I met you in the gym you had on sweatpants and an old T-shirt. I noticed you right away. You thought you were blending in but you had no idea how smoking hot you are. You walked right by me on the treadmill and I tripped."

"I remember that part. But what did you think when you first noticed me?" she asked. "Did you think I should let my hair down? That it was a shame I didn't do anything with my appearance?"

"I liked the way you walk." Cole's eyes took on a carnal gleam. "How you moved. It was powerful and sensual. I couldn't stop watching you."

Angie felt the heat crawl up her neck. She wasn't expecting that. Most people saw what she lacked. How she could improve and what a makeover could do for her. Cole saw something else.

"What about now?" she challenged. "Do you think I'm sexy in this suit?"

"You can't hide from me, Angie." His voice was a rasp. "Not even in that jacket."

Angie shivered and she buttoned up the jacket. She wasn't sure if she liked hearing that. "It's not that bad. I like it. It's comfortable."

"Wear whatever you want," he said. "It won't stop me from remembering how you feel underneath me, hot and naked."

"Stop it. Someone might hear you." She looked around and caught Cheryl's eye.

"I know what you look like when you're going wild. For me," he said, his tone thick with satisfaction. "Go ahead and hide. But know that I'm imagining peeling those clothes off you, layer by layer."

"Cheryl is coming this way. Behave," she pleaded. "Stop looking at me like you want to pin me against this wall and have your wicked way with me."

Cole's smile was slow and sexy. "Now there's a thought...."

"Have you seen Robin?" Cheryl asked as she tapped her pen against her small clipboard. "She's supposed to make a speech before we show the video of Brittany's college years."

"She went to flirt with Tim," Cole told her. Angie could feel his gaze on her. She adjusted the high collar that suddenly felt coarse and confining.

Cheryl glanced over at the groomsmen. "No, they said they haven't seen her."

"She was complaining about a headache," Angie said. "Something about having too much to drink. I'll go see if she's in the bathroom."

"Oh, you don't have to," Cheryl said, trying to stop her. "You're a guest."

"I know but you have so many other things on your to-do list," Angie replied. "It's not a problem." It would also allow her to break the spell that Cole was weaving around her. He was too close. He saw things about her she wanted to keep hidden.

Angie hurried out of the room and looked around for the restroom. She saw the sign and turned, bumping into her friend Steven.

"Hey, Angie," he greeted, his voice loud and slightly slurred. "Can you believe Patrick is going to be married tomorrow?"

Angie watched in horror when she saw Steven's chin wobble as tears formed in his eyes. "Steven, keep it together."

"He'll be the first of us to get married." He flung his arm around her shoulders and she staggered from his weight. "I never thought that would really happen."

"I'm surprised that a woman is marrying Patrick on purpose," Angie said as she tried to push Steven to stand on his own, "but I guess we underestimated him."

"Sssh." His fingers fumbled over her mouth. "I could have sworn you would be the first to marry in our group."

"Because I'm a female and therefore dream of weddings?" she asked. She never daydreamed about a wedding ceremony. She had no interest in dresses and tiaras.

"I thought you and Cole would make it down the aisle," Steven said as he clumsily patted her head. "Angie and Cole, sitting in a tree…first comes love, then comes marriage, then comes…something…how does it go?"

Angie gritted her teeth. This was why she hated weddings. "Steven, I'm never getting married. I'm not catching the bouquet so don't try to push me into the line of fire tomorrow. And if you keep saying that I'm the next one to get married, I will put you in a head-lock."

"I should put Cole in a headlock," he grumbled.

She propped Steven against the wall. "Leave Cole alone. Promise?"

"Just one punch?" Steven wagged a finger at her. "He broke your heart last time. He's going to do it again."

Angie sighed deeply. Her friends were only protecting her. They had no idea that Cole just wanted to be friends. The anger bubbled up inside her. She was so tired of being one of the guys. "Okay, fine. One punch."

"What?" Cole's voice was right behind her.

Angie jumped and looked around to see Cole's incredulous expression. "What? You have nothing to worry about. Steven's never been in a fight in his life."

"So you don't just hate weddings," Cole said with

a look in his eyes that Angie couldn't identify. "It's marriage, too."

She wasn't ready to have this discussion. She hated being Brittany's bridesmaid and she was getting sick of this wedding, but she didn't hate the idea of weddings. Not really.

Angie believed in love and marriage. True, she never thought about it for herself until she met Cole. She wanted to make a lifelong commitment with him, but she also knew now that he would never marry or settle into a family life. Okay, he could commit to her but he still bore the scars of his childhood. Cole Foster was the only man she wanted to marry but that wasn't going to happen no matter how much she wished for it.

"Cole, can you make sure Steven gets back to the rehearsal dinner? His sense of direction isn't that great even when he's sober." She didn't stop to see if Cole would agree. "Steven, have you seen Robin? The maid of honor?" she added, given her friend's confused expression.

"Yeah, wow." Steven shook his head. "She can't hold her liquor."

"What are you talking about?" Cole asked. "We just saw her and she was fine."

"She was making a play for me. Then her face got all red and blotchy. She clutched her throat."

"Like she was choking?" Angie asked.

"No. I assumed she was going to throw up. I saw her stagger into the bathroom." Steven pointed at the door down the hall.

"I should check on her," Angie told Cole as she rushed to the bathroom. She wasn't sure why she was so worried. Robin was getting sick. It happens. No big deal.

But she couldn't suppress the alarm that was shooting through her veins. Angie mentally braced herself before she pushed open the door. "Robin? Are you doing okay?"

Angie froze when she saw Robin sprawled on the bathroom floor.

15

COLE STOOD BEHIND Angie as they watched the paramedics wheel Robin away on a stretcher. Angie had taken care of Robin and now looked as if she were going to collapse herself. He knew how she felt.

"Are you okay?" he asked Angie softly as he put his arms around her. "You're shaking like a leaf."

"I'm fine. It's just the adrenaline." She stuffed her hands in her pockets. "It'll go away soon."

"You did great," he said. "She's going to recover."

He had been impressed in how Angie jumped into action. He had raced to her when she called out. There had been something in the way she'd called his name. It shook him to the core and all he could think about was getting to Angie. He wanted to protect her and take over.

But by the time he stepped into the bathroom, Angie had already taken an EpiPen out of Robin's small purse. Without any hesitation, she had jabbed the needle in the maid of honor's thigh. She had continued with the rescue breathing while he phoned for an ambulance. Angie was shaking now but she had been focused and thorough during the crisis. It was one of the many things he admired about her.

He heard the piercing siren start and saw the ambulance's lights as the vehicle sped away. "How did you even know she needed an epinephrine injection?" he asked.

"She said something about food allergies when she was at the hospital café." Angie rested her head against his shoulder and didn't protest when he stroked her hair. "I know Steven thought she was drunk but we had just seen her and she had complained of a headache. I figured something was off when he described the symptoms but I didn't think about an allergic reaction until I saw her on the floor."

"I wondered what was in the hors d'oeuvres," he said as they walked slowly back to the dining room. It was eerily quiet compared to the festive spirit of a mere few minutes ago. Now the video was turned off and the guests were milling aimlessly in the entryway and parking lot. "Where was Robin going to sit?"

"There." Angie pointed at the empty seat. "The maid of honor was going to sit next to the groom."

He stared at the place setting. There was a wet ring on the tablecloth from where her pink martini had been. "Where's her drink? She had set it down when she got the headache."

"She was almost finished with it," Angie said. She stepped away from him and picked up Robin's place card from the table. "I'm sure the waiting staff removed it."

Cole wasn't so sure. "Do you remember how she said it tasted differently?"

"The recipe isn't hard science." Her fingers continued to tremble as she set the card down. "The bartender here could have used a different bubble gum. I'm sure she ate an hors d'oeuvre and didn't know the ingredients."

"No, she was careful. I saw her," he said as he examined the other tables. Most of the guests still had their drinks next to their place cards.

"I can't believe this is happening," Brittany said as she stormed into the room with Cheryl and Patrick trailing behind her. Her face was mottled red and her hair was falling out of its neat twist. Cole felt the anger come off her in waves.

"What was Robin allergic to?" Cole asked Brittany.

Brittany stepped back abruptly and gave him a strange look. As if she had already forgotten about Robin's situation. "How should I know? Am I supposed to know every food restriction and allergy of every guest?"

"I'm sure she mentioned it when she had to choose her meals for the dinners."

Brittany crossed her arms and thrust out her chin. "What are you trying to say?"

"Peanuts," Cheryl interrupted. "It was on the card when she RSVP'd. She's very allergic to peanuts. There couldn't be any cross-contamination in the kitchen."

"See?" Angie told Cole. "Accidents happen."

He knew what Angie was trying to tell him. He shouldn't waste his time and pursue the incident like he did with Heidi's fall. But he couldn't let it go. "Accidents are happening a lot with this wedding."

"They certainly are," Brittany said as she stood in front of them. Her legs were braced for a fight and her hands were on her hips. Her cream lace dress was pale compared to her flushed face. "And they always seem to happen when Angie is around."

Angie rolled her shoulders back and cast a stern glare at Brittany. "Are you saying I'm bad luck?"

"I think you're trying to sabotage my wedding." The guests gasped at Brittany's suggestion and started to whisper.

Cole felt the flare of anger. He saw Angie's lips part in shock. And he saw Patrick standing behind his fiancée and saying nothing. Cole was ready to step in and fight for Angie's honor, but Angie held out her hand and stopped him.

"Why would I do that?" Angie asked coldly.

"Oh, I don't know." Brittany's eyes glittered with rage. "Because you want Patrick for yourself."

Angie looked at Brittany as if the bride had lost her mind. "He's not my type." She gave her friend a quick look of apology. "No offense, Patrick."

"Angie has never been interested in Patrick," Tim interjected. "I always thought she wasn't into men until she hooked up with Cole."

"Thanks, Tim, but I can take it from here," Angie said without looking at him.

"I know you don't like me," Brittany said in a hiss. "You're jealous because you're not the first person Patrick calls anymore. You've been downgraded and you can't stand it."

"You're wrong, Brittany. I don't care about that."

"Then it's because you hate weddings," Brittany growled. "You've made that very clear."

Cole wanted to defend Angie. Yes, she hated weddings. It took him by surprise, too. Her declaration unsettled him and he wasn't sure why. She had a traditional streak that he loved. She wasn't the type to flip through bridal magazines or cry during the exchange of rings. But she respected the vows and she upheld the values that were symbolized in weddings.

Although that didn't stop Angie from hating this wedding, it seemed, and he didn't judge her for it. She was trying to be supportive to her friend. No one noticed that she wouldn't do otherwise for a friend. She would stand up for Patrick and defend his decision in a wife, even if he were making a huge mistake in marrying this woman.

"Angie was just saying she hated weddings," Steven said. "And marriage, too."

Cole closed his eyes and reined in his temper before he reached out and silenced Angie's friend. At least the guys were sort of helping her, unlike Patrick.

"See?" Brittany crossed her arms as if to say she had proved her point. "There you go."

"I have been nothing but obliging about your wedding." Angie took a step forward but stopped when Cole placed his hand on her shoulder. He knew her emotions were all over the place and that she could react unpredictably. "I have done everything you asked of me."

"Then why do all these 'accidents,'" sputtered Brittany, who was using air quotes, "and disasters happen when you're around?"

"Because I'm required to be at every event," Angie said calmly with a hint of real bitterness. "Every meeting, every fitting and every shower."

"I wish you didn't have to be. I knew you were trouble, but I had no choice." Brittany gestured wildly at her fiancé. "Patrick wanted you in the bridal party and I certainly wasn't going to let you be the best man."

"Brittany…" Patrick said, but his warning had no

conviction. Cole knew Patrick would take Brittany's side, even if his bride tore Angie's feelings to shreds.

"Having you in my bridal party changed everything," Brittany revealed to Angie. "Heidi and Robin weren't my first choice of bridesmaids. I had to ask them so we could work around your coloring and your body type."

"That's not my fault," Angie said. "And who picks a bridesmaid based on their hair color? That's ridiculous."

Brittany wasn't listening. "And now my maid of honor is hospitalized? Again? That can't be a coincidence." She clenched her fists at her sides and stood toe-to-toe with Angie. Angie refused to back down.

"Patrick," Cole said as he watched Brittany vibrate with anger. "Get her away from Angie or I will." And he wouldn't be gentle when protecting Angie.

"Relax, Brittany," Angie said as she met the bride's hateful gaze. "I'm sure Robin will be fine for tomorrow's ceremony."

"But what if she isn't?" Brittany poked her finger against Angie's shoulder. "You've ruined everything."

"That's enough." Cole stood between Angie and Brittany. He wasn't about to allow this to escalate into a fistfight. "Angie didn't do this. I was with her."

Brittany snorted at his claim. "I'm supposed to take the word of a stripper?"

Cole's nostrils flared. He wanted to tell Brittany that he was a former police detective and a private investigator. Most people would accept him as a credible witness and a solid alibi.

"Then take the word of the groomsman," Angie said. "Take the ushers' word. They all know me. They will vouch for me."

Tim and Steven stared at each other and then looked away. "I need to use the bathroom," Tim said as he darted for the door.

"Me, too," Steven muttered as he backed away from the group.

"Seriously, guys?" Angie asked.

"And why does Brittany think Cole is a stripper? Wait up, Tim," Steven said as he sprinted after his friend.

"Come on, Brittany," Cheryl cooed in a soothing voice as she cautiously touched her boss's elbow. "Let's have you sit down and get something to drink."

Brittany gave Angie one last hateful look before she allowed her assistant to lead her to an empty table.

Cole grabbed Patrick's arm to keep him from following. "I need to talk to you."

"Dude, I'm sorry about Brittany," he said in a low voice and looked over at his fiancée. "I'll talk to her. She's upset and she doesn't know what she's saying. Angie is still in the wedding."

"No," Cole said. "I don't want her in the wedding."

"I'm right here, guys," Angie said as she stood next to them. "Rather than talking about me, try talking *to* me."

"I'm serious." Cole glanced to where Brittany and her assistant were sitting. "Someone is trying to take out the bridesmaids, one by one. Angie is next."

Patrick's mouth twisted with displeasure. "You don't know that."

"You have two injured bridesmaids," Cole pointed out. "What are the odds?"

"Maids of honor," Angie said, correcting him. She shrugged when he and Patrick looked down at her. "They got hurt when they were maids of honor."

"That's crazy," Patrick said. "Who would do something like that?"

"I don't know." But Cole had his suspicions. He hoped he was wrong.

Patrick's features tightened with anger. "Do you realize what you're saying? The only people at this party are my friends and family."

Angie glanced at Cole. "He catches on a lot faster than Brittany."

"These were accidents," Patrick whispered fiercely. "Do not share your theories with Brittany. The last thing I need is a paranoid bride."

Cole sensed that Patrick was listening. He just didn't want to hear it. Didn't want to believe it. "Keep an eye on her," Cole suggested. "I don't know if someone has it in for Brittany or if it has something to do with the bridesmaids."

"I'm not supposed to see the bride until the wedding." Patrick rubbed his hands over his face. "Stupid tradition." He paused and looked hopefully at Angie.

"Oh, no." Angie shook her head. "That is so not going to happen. I will not be the bride's babysitter. She already thinks I'm trouble."

"Besides, I'm watching Angie tonight," Cole added.

Angie gave him a look of surprise. "No, you're not."

"I'm taking you back to my apartment."

"I have to report to Brittany's after the dinner. It's some sort of final bridal send-off, although it sounds like a bait and switch. I suspect I'll be roped into making hundreds of party favors for most of the night."

"Forget it." He didn't want Angie to be around anyone from this group. She would be trapped and defenseless if someone attempted to harm her.

She put her hands on her hips. "I can't. Brittany is

already mad at me. If I skip this last event, it will send her over the edge."

"I admit she's upset," Patrick said. "But everything about this wedding is going wrong. Fine, you guys deal with this on your own, I need to take care of Brittany."

Cole nodded and waited until Patrick was some distance away from them. "Angie, listen to me."

"I'm okay," Angie insisted. "No one is targeting me."

"You don't know that for sure." She was the last bridesmaid and would probably be promoted to be maid of honor. The wedding was tomorrow and the person doing all this would have to act fast.

"Think about it, Cole. Heidi and Robin went to the same school and the same sorority. They are friends with Brittany. I have nothing in common with them."

"Other than being a bridesmaid."

She gave a huff of exasperation, refusing to agree with the obvious. "We already decided what happened to Heidi was an accident."

"But now a pattern is emerging."

Angie scoffed at him. "Two accidents do not make a pattern."

He wasn't going to wait for the third. "I want to play it safe."

"Heidi had a head injury." She splayed one hand. "Robin had an allergic reaction." She splayed out her other hand. "Each accident is different."

"But they both look like accidents."

"All right," she said through clenched teeth. "I will be extra cautious tonight and tomorrow. Okay?"

"Not good enough," Cole said. "Whoever is doing this won't take any chances. They'll make sure you can't be at the ceremony."

Angie sighed and smoothed her hands over her hair as she tried to decide what to do. "Do you still think it's Brittany?" she asked in a low voice.

"No, not anymore."

She looked around the restaurant. "Who do you think it is?"

He hesitated. He wanted to tell Angie his suspicions so she would be wary, but he knew Angie would act on any information he gave her. She would pursue instead of retreat. "I'm not sure."

Angie narrowed her eyes. "Yes, you are. Tell me."

"Cheryl."

"Cheryl?" She glanced over at where the assistant was sitting. Cheryl was huddled with Brittany and Patrick. The conversation looked serious.

"Think about it," Cole said. "She's at all the events but in the background."

"She's too loyal to her boss to sabotage Brittany's wedding."

"Maybe she's not trying to stop the wedding," he argued. "She could think she's protecting Brittany from Heidi and Robin. I'm sure she knows all about how miserable they made her in college. Or she's showing how indispensible she is to Brittany."

"That's possible." Angie bit down on her bottom lip as she considered his argument. "She's in charge of all the details."

"And she is in the perfect position to clear away any evidence." Cole motioned at Robin's place setting.

"Brittany doesn't strike me as the kind of woman who picks up after herself," Angie muttered. Her shoulders tensed. "Uh-oh."

"What?" He placed a protective hand on her arm.

"Patrick is coming this way," she said via the side

of her mouth, "and he's got that look on his face. That is not a good look."

"Angie?" Patrick looked away and nervously rubbed his hand over his mouth. "I really hate to tell you this. I'm sure it's temporary. Just until Brittany calms down."

"Just spit it out, Patrick."

Patrick took a big breath. "Brittany wants you to leave," he said in a rush.

Angie showed no emotion and gave a short nod. "I can do that. Not a problem."

"And..." Patrick's face turned bright red. "You're banned from the wedding."

16

"Banned!" Angie shouted as she entered her apartment. She threw her keys on the small table by the door. "Me? *I'm* banned?"

"I know," Cole said as he followed her into the loft. He closed the door and leaned against it as he watched Angie pace. "You've been chanting that since we left."

"Banned!" She ripped off her jacket and threw it on the ground. "No one bans Angela Lawson. No one!"

"Brittany has." He pointed out as he watched her kick off her shoes.

Angie balled her hands into fists. "The nerve of that woman."

"It's not just Brittany. Patrick is backing her up." He hated to mention it but he felt it was necessary. Patrick was going to take Brittany's side from now on. Angie needed to adapt or risk losing her friend.

"Can you believe it?" She furiously tugged at her ponytail and a second later her hair tumbled free. Cole noted the long tresses as they fell around her neck and shoulders. "He has known me for twenty years. And he sides with that woman."

"I'm sure everything will be cleared up and all will be forgiven," he murmured, distracted at how soft and shiny her hair looked. His stomach clenched as he remembered how it felt against his hand and how it swept down his body when Angie was on top.

"Oh, no." She pointed at Cole. "I am not forgiving her. Or Patrick. And to think I bought them a good wedding present."

"Look at the big picture," he suggested, thrusting his hands in his pockets as he watched Angie's angry strides. "You don't have to be a bridesmaid anymore."

She stopped and turned around, her hands on her hips again. "Why aren't you angry? My best friend just kicked me out of his wedding."

"I'm happy you're out of the line of fire."

"Nothing was going to happen to me," she insisted, walking up to him. "But don't you want to go find out if Cheryl is behind this?"

"I can't prove she did any of it," he said, quietly watching the emotions flicker in Angie's eyes. "I have no motive and no weapon. The woman is smart."

She didn't budge an inch. "I bet you she's been poisoning Brittany's mind about me. It's because we've been asking questions."

"Or Brittany just doesn't like you."

Angie nodded as she considered that. "Yeah, there's that, too." She clucked her tongue. "You know, she was right. I am envious."

"What?" His heart stopped as jealousy, hot and bitter, seized his rib cage.

She gave him a curious look. "Not because she has Patrick. Oh, God, no."

"Good to know." He was tempted to rub his knuckles against his chest to ease the pain. "Then what?"

"I'm envious about what she and Patrick have." She looked away as a bittersweet smile tugged at her mouth. "You and I used to have that. I miss it. I miss having you in my life."

"I'm here." He wasn't going anywhere. But would she believe that?

Angie narrowed her eyes as she looked at the door. "You know what? I'm going to crash it."

"Crash what? The ceremony?" Was she kidding? Please let her be kidding. But he saw the look in her eye and the stubborn tilt of her chin.

"That's right." She pumped her fist. "No one can keep me from my friend's wedding."

"I can," he said. His harsh tone caught her notice.

Angie watched him carefully. "You won't."

"I'm looking after you until this wedding is over." He cupped his hands on her stiff shoulders and made her face away from the door. She protested as he pushed her farther into the room. "Consider me your personal bodyguard."

"I don't need one."

She dragged her bare feet on the floor but it wasn't enough resistance to keep him from moving her. "I'll decide that."

"I'm not a bridesmaid anymore," she said, the anger evaporating from her voice. "I'll be fine."

"We're assuming this is related to the wedding," he said as he stopped next to the bed. "It could be for a different reason. I'm not taking any chances."

She sighed. "Go home, Cole."

He shook his head. "Not unless you're coming with me."

"I can take care of myself." Her voice was quiet but steady.

"I know." Angie was strong and capable. She knew it and so did he. Yet he wanted to help her. He wanted to be there for her and prove to her that she wasn't on her own. "But I want to take care of you, too. If anything happens to you…"

"Cole, I've had a bad day." She rubbed her hands over her face. "I'm tired, I'm upset and you need to go before I do something stupid. Like lose my temper. Or cry. At this moment, it could be both."

Did she not want to show that side of herself? Was she worried he would leave if she showed too much emotion? "Go ahead. Let it all out. I don't mind."

"You don't get it, do you?" She met his gaze. "My restraint is almost gone. I don't want to lean on a friend tonight. I want something more. I want everything."

He tried to squelch down the hope building inside him. "What are you saying?"

"I can't be friends with you. Not anymore."

The hope instantly transformed into panic. What did he do wrong? He had been on his best behavior. Whatever she needed, he would do it. Anything to keep her in his life. "Why not?" he asked gruffly.

"I need more from you." She flattened her hand against his chest. "I need to know that you're there for me no matter what."

He swallowed hard, not sure if he heard correctly. "I'm with you all the way." Even if she gave up on him, even if she moved on. He would be there for her whenever she needed him. She didn't have to ask.

"You have always been the most important person in my life," she said. "And I knew that I was your top priority."

"You still are." She put him above everyone else.

In some ways he knew that. She showed it in every choice she made.

"It's not enough," she said. "I want it all back. I want to share my life with you. Have a future together."

This was more than he'd ever expected. He was afraid to make a move. If he said or did something, he could break the spell.

"I get that you can't make a commitment." She slid her hands up his chest and looped them behind his neck. "After the hell you went through…I understand that now. But I don't want to be mere friends. Or friends with benefits."

He was certain that she could feel his heart beating hard. "You want another try."

She nodded. "I want what we had, Cole. I'm not going to ask for anything more, but I refuse to ask for anything less."

He cautiously wrapped his arms around her waist and drew her closer. "Are you sure?"

"I love you, Cole." Her voice was clear and full of confidence. "I haven't stopped loving you."

He couldn't look away from her eyes. "How can you? When all I've ever done is disappoint you."

She pressed her lips against his. "I asked too much of you."

"No, you haven't." His hands shook as he caressed her back. "Tell me what you want and I'll get it for you. Your happiness means everything to me."

"You know what would make me happy right now? If you took me to bed. Let me show you how much I love you."

"No, Angie," he said as he began to unbutton her shirt. "Let me show you how good we can be together."

COLE REMOVED HER clothes in record time. She stood before him naked and aroused, throbbing with desire as he reached for her. She gasped in surprise when he playfully tossed her onto the bed.

"Come here," Angie said, her arms outstretched.

"Soon," he replied as he discarded his jacket. She noticed his hands were unsteady as he undid the buttons on his cuffed sleeves.

"Let me help you," she offered as she moved to rise.

"No." Cole slipped off one shoe and then the other. "Start without me."

Her eyes widened. "What?"

His darkened expression reflected pure passion. "Touch yourself," his said in a husky voice, "and let me watch."

Her breath hitched in her throat. "Do you mean like this?" she asked as she cupped her breasts and pushed them together.

"Yeah," he said roughly as he dragged off his socks. "Just like that."

"But I like it best when you touch me like this," she said as she rubbed her palms over her nipples. "It feels so good."

"What else feels good?" he asked as he clumsily yanked off his tie.

"When you do this." She pinched her nipple and the heat, thick and addictive, scorched through her veins. She moaned and arched her spine to accommodate the flash of pleasure.

"I didn't catch that," Cole said as he unbuttoned his shirt. His teasing tone didn't match the tension vibrating in him. Or the way his skin tightened against his features. He was getting aroused, hard and fast, as he watched her.

"It was something like this." She pinched her nipples harder. Angie gasped from the tingling sensations and rolled her hips. She focused on Cole through hooded eyes and her skin prickled when she noted the raw lust in his gaze.

"What else do you like?" he asked as he tugged his shirt off.

"Hmm…" She glided her hands along her chest and neck before sinking her fingers into her long hair. The warmth had invaded her body. Her arms and legs felt heavy. Her breasts felt large and full. And her hips…

"Show me," Cole commanded. His hands on his belt buckle.

She smiled, boldly, as she skimmed her hands along her sides. One hand stayed on her pelvic bone before she splayed her fingers over her mound.

"What would you like me to do?" he asked as he slowly unbuckled his belt.

She felt a wave of shyness and hesitated. Cole seemed mesmerized by her brazenness, but she didn't want to be too aggressive. She knew better than to ask for too much.

"Angie," Cole said as he slowly unzipped his pants. "I want to know. Don't hide from me."

She didn't want to. Not anymore. Hiding caused misunderstandings and mistakes. It meant holding back when she wanted to live and love fully.

Her pulse raced as she slid one hand over the slick folds of her sex. She glided her fingers slowly as she watched Cole's reaction. And she raised her other hand over her head. She moaned, rocking her hips as the pleasure coiled tight in her belly.

"Oh, Cole." She drew out his name. "I want you deep inside me."

Without hesitation, he shoved off his remaining clothes. Angie couldn't help but be aware that he was rock hard and already breathing deeply.

"Take me now, Cole."

Instantly, he held the backs of her knees and pulled her toward him. Cole hooked her legs over his hips. Her bottom was raised and her hips tilted up. She was totally at his mercy.

He eagerly explored her body with his hands. "Like this?" he asked with a wicked smile as he palmed her breasts. She arched into his touch, enjoying the pressure and friction.

"Yes-s-s," she assured him. She bit her lip, holding back a deep groan as he teased her nipples. "More," she muttered as she moved her head from side to side.

"What about this?" He drew one hand down her abdomen and cupped her mound. Her heart skipped a beat at his possessive hold. She undulated when he pressed her swollen clit.

"I want everything," she said wildly. "I want it now."

Cole put his hands on her hips, his fingers holding tight as he surged into her welcoming heat. The breath stuttered from her throat as he filled her. Cole stilled and closed his eyes as he savored this moment.

Angie stretched her arms out, surrendering to him. Her body accepted Cole and drew him in deeper.

Cole shuddered as he tried to control his most primitive instincts. "No," he warned. "I want this to last."

"I can't help it," she said as she bucked against him. "I want you so much."

He let out a feral growl and sank into her. Heat blanketed her skin as each strong thrust went deep. She rocked against the bed, bunching the sheets in her hands as the pleasure rippled through her.

She watched Cole and saw the sweat gleam along his ruddy skin, his muscles straining each time he withdrew.

"I love you, Cole," she said as the burning, growing pressure inside her burst. She shut her eyes as the white-hot intensity of her orgasm claimed her. Again and again it came in crashing waves as Cole climaxed.

Angie kept her eyes closed. She wanted to remember this heightened moment, this all-consuming pleasure. But she couldn't ignore the fact that Cole didn't say any words of love. And while she felt protected and desired when she was with him, she knew he may never say those important words to her.

17

COLE STARED AT the small stone church as he got out of his car. It appeared quaint and picturesque but he knew danger lurked beneath bunches of white flowers and pink luminaries. Guests were already entering the building and he heard the strains of organ music from where he stood. He hoped he wasn't too late.

He fished his phone from his pocket and checked his messages. Nothing. He tried to take a deep breath but his chest was tight with worry. Cole punched the screen and redialed Angie's phone. He felt like throwing his phone when he immediately got her voice mail.

"Angie, why don't you have your phone on? Call me when you get this." He hung up and rubbed his aching head. When he found her, he was going to make sure she never left his side.

He grabbed his suit jacket and shoved his arms in the sleeves. His movements were choppy and forceful as the panic swelled inside him. Where was Angie? Why wasn't she picking up her phone? Was she hurt? Was her phone dead? Or was she ignoring his calls?

It was bad enough waking up alone in her apartment, but his stomach had made a sickening twist when he found her note explaining that she was back in the wedding.

Back as a bridesmaid, possibly as maid of honor. Either way, she was back to being a target.

His phone rang. Cole checked the screen and saw Angie's number. He felt weak, almost boneless, as the relief poured through him. He immediately answered. "Angie?"

"Hey, Cole," Angie replied cheerfully as if she didn't hear the urgency in his voice. "I'm sorry I missed your call. And your texts. All twelve of them."

"Where have you been?" he demanded.

"Didn't you get my note? I put it where I was sure you'd see it. I didn't want you to worry but I had to leave quickly this morning."

"Yes, I got the note," he said through clenched teeth as he straightened the knot of his necktie. "You should have taken me with you."

"I tried to wake you up. I really did, honest. I guess I wore you out."

He heard the smile in her voice but he wasn't amused. "What are you doing at the wedding? You were banned."

"Patrick texted me early this morning. He and Brittany want me to be in the ceremony." She lowered her voice. "I have a feeling it's really Patrick who wants me there but—"

"Why did you accept?" The frustration rang in his voice and he didn't care.

"Patrick is my friend," she reminded him, "and I know he fought hard to keep me in the wedding. What else could I say?"

"I can think of a few things just off the top of my

head. For instance, the bride has it in for you." He ignored the woman in the floppy hat who gave him a sharp look. "And her assistant is bumping off bridesmaids."

Angie scoffed. "We don't know that."

"Also, Patrick should never have allowed Brittany to speak to you in that manner," Cole continued as he took the steps to the church two at a time. "You tore up your bridesmaid dress in a fit of rage and can't possibly participate...."

"I would never destroy this dress no matter how trashy it is," Angie said breezily. "You have no idea how much it cost."

He entered the church and looked around the vestibule. He saw a few guests. The men wore dark suits while the women looked like exotic birds with their brightly colored dresses and oddly shaped hats. He didn't see Angie. "Where are you?"

"I'm outside the bridal room. We're still getting Brittany ready for the ceremony. It's not going well. The woman is on the verge of a breakdown."

Cole frowned as the phone connection crackled. "We?"

"Robin is here. The hospital released her late last night." He heard the relief in Angie's voice. "She doesn't have a lot of energy and she looks really pale, but she's determined to see this through."

"That's great," Cole said. "I'm glad she's okay."

"She must really want to be in this wedding," Angie said. "I think they want me here as backup if Robin can't perform her maid-of-honor duties."

"Where is Cheryl?" he asked as he went down a hallway, hoping it was in the direction of the bridal room.

"Handling some detail with the minister. You don't

have to worry about me. She's too busy to plot my demise."

"I will always worry about you."

"That's sweet," she declared in a soft voice. "I want you to know I wasn't ignoring you. I'm not sure why I didn't get your messages. The connection here must be weak."

"I've been looking for you everywhere. And—" He turned the corner and spotted her alone, leaning against the wall. Cole stopped as his heart gave a violent lurch. "Holy..."

Angie wore the most provocative dress. It faithfully followed every line and curve of her body. It was designed to gain a man's attention.

"Cole." Her expression brightened when she saw him and turned off her phone.

He strode toward her and gathered her close. It felt good to have her in his arms. "You are in so much trouble."

"For what?" she asked as she held on to him. "For not answering my phone?"

For the phone. For not listening to him. And definitely for the dress. He took a step back and stared at her. The dress was shiny and a strange shade of green, but it fit her perfectly. The low-cut dress hugged her pert breasts and thrust them out like an offering. The skirt clung to her hips and was perilously short. It would ride up her legs and would draw every male's attention to her bottom when she walked.

"That dress," he said slowly.

She pulled away and crossed her arms. "Trashy, isn't it."

"No." He grabbed her wrists and held her arms out

as he took a longer look. The dress emphasized her breasts and hips. "You look…wow."

"Stop teasing me." She tried to escape his hold but he wouldn't let her.

"I'm serious. Wear this dress for me some time," he asked as his gaze lingered on her long, bare legs. He saw the delicate high heels and changed his mind. "Forget that. Just wear the shoes and nothing else."

He saw a naughty gleam in her eyes before she dipped her head. "No way."

"Why not?" Cole asked as he held her hands above her head. Her breasts threatened to spill out of her dress and she tilted her hips as he leaned into her. She was soft and yielding as her body cradled his. Desire for her pulsed right through him and he grew hard as stone.

"This is not me," she insisted.

"Yes, it is." He glanced around the hallway, wondering where he could whisk her away.

"No, it's not," she said in a biting tone. "I can't pull this look off. Do you know me at all?"

"I know every side and every facet of you," he said as he lowered his arms and caressed her cheek. "This is you. It was you last night."

"I would never choose this dress. It's too revealing. Too sexy. It promises something I can't deliver."

"You are sexy." His voice was rough and low as he brushed his knuckles down her throat. "It's driving me wild."

She gave him a skeptical look. "I thought I was sexy in sweatpants and an oversize T-shirt."

"You are. Because that's when you feel confident and comfortable. Because you can hide in those clothes." He cupped her breast and shuddered as the lust whipped through him. "You can't hide in this."

"Don't tell me that," she said, smiling and thrust her breast into his hand. "That's the last thing I need to hear before I walk down the aisle."

He let go of her and gave the dress another look. "How do you get out of this?" he asked as he licked his lips with anticipation.

Angie flattened her hands against his chest. "Don't even try."

"I'm surprised Brittany is allowing you to wear this," he muttered as he crushed the skirt with his hand. "You're going to upstage the bride."

"I look like a joke."

He hooked his finger under her chin and tilted her head up, forcing her to look into his eyes. "Angie, you don't need a dress to show that you are a beautiful and sexy woman. But don't think you have to hide in sweatpants because you're afraid of being noticed."

"Cole, you don't understand." She brushed his hand away from her face. "What you see is hours of work from a team of professionals. This is as good as it gets. And I don't… It's not…"

"I see you. The real you. Behind the makeup and… what the hell is this?" He rubbed his fingers together. "Glitter?"

"Yeah." Angie said roughly as her chest rose and fell as she drew in each breath.

He bumped his forehead with hers and stared into her eyes. "Hide as much as you want, but it's a waste of time. I don't care if you are walking down a runway or limping across the finish line. I will always see you as a strong and sexy woman."

She lowered her lashes as her cheeks turned pink. "Cole…"

He didn't want her to feel shy. He wanted Angie to

feel safe with him. "Just know that you don't have to hide from me."

The loud creak of a door echoed in the empty hallway. Angie was startled at the sound and looked in the direction of the bridal room.

"Oh, my God. Really?" Robin said and planted her hands on her hips. "Cole, do not smudge her makeup or wrinkle her dress. In fact, do not touch her at all."

Cole raised his hands in surrender and took a step back. He noticed Robin wore the same dress as Angie. He didn't spare a second glance at the maid of honor. Angie was a living, breathing fantasy.

Angie sighed and turned her attention to the maid of honor. "What do you want, Robin?"

Robin pointed at the door she just exited. "I'm having trouble tying the corset in Brittany's gown. I need help. I need muscle."

"And you thought of me," she said. "I'll be right there."

"Good," she said as she returned through the same doorway. "I swear, I can't turn my back on you for a second."

"I'm sorry, Cole. I have to go." She bit her bottom lip and gave him a hopeful look beneath her lashes. "Are you going to attend the wedding?"

"Yes." He grabbed her hand and raised it to his mouth. Brushing his lips against her knuckles, he promised, "I'm here for you."

"Why isn't it fitting?" Brittany shrieked. She stretched the corset one way and then another, and pressed it to her stomach. "I swear this dress fit perfectly two days ago."

"Breathe in," Robin suggested.

"I haven't eaten solid foods for a week," Brittany swore as tears sparkled in her eyes. "I didn't cheat once. Not once! This should fit."

"It will," Robin promised. "Don't cry or we'll have to redo your makeup. Angie, how's it going back there?"

"Are you pulling as hard as you can?" Brittany asked.

"Yes," she said through gritted teeth as she pulled the pink ribbons that crisscrossed in the back of the corset. The mermaid gown was of the palest pink but there was nothing innocent about the dress. The plunging neckline and flared hips dramatically accentuated Brittany's curves. Angie didn't know how Brittany was going to breathe, let alone walk.

Angie pulled so hard she thought she would get rope burn but the corset didn't budge. "I'm afraid to pull any harder," she said. "I don't want the dress to rip."

"Rip?" Brittany whirled around and gave Angie a hateful look. "What did you do to my dress?"

"Nothing!" Angie said as she rubbed her reddened hands. "The dress is fine."

"Stay away from me." Brittany teetered on her heels as she took a cautious step back. "I don't want you touching my dress."

Angie looked at Robin. "I give up."

"Where is Cheryl?" Brittany asked as she examined the back of her dress in the mirror. "Why isn't she here helping me?"

Robin shrugged. "I haven't seen her since we arrived at the church."

"Call her," Brittany ordered. "Call her right now."

"I have." Robin flopped into a seat next to the bride

and held her head in her hands. "Constantly. I don't think we get cell reception here."

"Go find her," Brittany screamed. "She'll know what to do."

"I'll do that," Angie volunteered. She'll do anything that didn't require her to be locked in a room with Brittany.

"Hurry," Robin pleaded. She looked at the clock. "We don't have much time before the ceremony starts."

Angie hurried out of the room with Brittany's wails ringing in her ears. She took a few quick steps before she stumbled and tripped on her heels. Angie grimaced as she twisted her ankle. She pressed her lips together as the pain shot through her leg.

It didn't seem to matter that she had practiced walking in the shoes for hours, Angie decided as she limped down the hallway. It was practically guaranteed that she was going to trip as she made her way down the aisle.

No, she won't. Angie rolled her shoulders back and held up her chin. She could master these shoes. She could wear this dress. She wasn't about to be nervous over the height of her hemline or heels. All she had to do was find Cole and concentrate on him while she came down the aisle. When he looked at her with a mix of awe and desire, she would find her confidence.

Angie saw an open door that led out to the church garden. "Cheryl?" she called. "Are you out here?"

"Yes." Cheryl appeared from behind a flowering bush. "I'm getting the place ready for the photographer."

"Brittany needs you." Angie watched Cheryl and frowned when she noticed the assistant wore the same shoes as the bridesmaids. She even had the same polish on her toes. It was bubble-gum-pink. Yet Cheryl didn't get a pedicure with the rest of the bridal party.

"What seems to be the problem?" Cheryl asked as she walked up the stone steps.

"There's a problem with the dress," Angie replied. She narrowed her eyes when she noticed Cheryl's dress. The assistant wore a soft pink cardigan but her outfit was shiny and green. It was a replica of the bridesmaids' dresses.

Cheryl stopped at the top of the steps. Angie dragged her gaze up, cataloging every detail. She was belatedly aware that Cheryl was studying her closely.

"Did you forget something?" Angie asked, doing her best to seem casual as her instincts were sensing trouble.

"I only have to do one more thing…." Cheryl suddenly reached out with both hands and pushed Angie down the steps.

18

ANGIE LUNGED OUT to grab onto Cheryl, but instead, tumbled to the ground. The rough stone steps scratched her skin. Angie wasted no time, though, before she leaped to her feet where she'd landed. She felt every cut and bruise, but she tried to ignore the pain as she focused on Cheryl.

"Damn," Cheryl groaned. She stood at the top of the steps with her hands on her hips. "What are you? A ninja?"

"So, I'm next, huh?" Angie asked as she held on to the arm that had broken her fall. She rubbed it as she scanned the garden. She didn't see a way out. "I'm surprised that you're not trying to finish the job on Robin."

Cheryl's eyes widened with surprise. "You figured it out that it was me." Cheryl gave a mocking clap. "Well done, Angie. You are not the dumb jock Brittany claims you are."

"Why are you doing this to Brittany?" Angie asked. She looked at the hedges that bordered the garden. They were too tall to climb over. "I thought you cared for her."

"I *do* care." Cheryl's face turned red with anger. "I've done everything to give her the wedding she wanted. I care more than anyone in her bridal party. I probably care more than Patrick and it's his wedding."

"Okay, calm down." Angie looked around and considered her options. She didn't have her cell phone, and even if she did, it probably wouldn't work. Everyone was in the church except for Robin and Brittany. Angie's only hope was that Robin would come looking for her. But what were the chances that she'd find her in the enclosed garden? No one would see her before Cheryl attacked again. Her only plan was to keep Cheryl talking until someone became concerned for them.

"I am calm," Cheryl retorted.

"That's true," she said as she took another step back. Maybe she could rush Cheryl and tackle her. But that probably wouldn't work in her favor. "You have nerves of steel. Like when you hit Heidi at the strip club. Did you plan that or was it a spur-of-the-moment kind of thing?"

"I don't know why she asked Heidi to be maid of honor." Cheryl scoffed and rolled her eyes. "Brittany thought she would do whatever we asked, but it turns out the woman was useless. Her ineptitude was going to ruin the wedding. Heidi needed to be told what to do, how to do it and when it needed to be done. It made my job twice as hard."

"I'm sure it did." Angie nodded her head vigorously as she took another step back. "So you had to get her out of the wedding?"

"No, that was a bonus." Cheryl took the next step. "I was reminding her of her duties and she went off on me. She was complaining about how much work was involved."

"Didn't she realize that this was an honor?" Angie asked and realized Cheryl didn't hear her sarcasm.

"She made me so angry," Cheryl growled. "I have worked on this wedding for months and I wasn't paid for the extra time. I did all this while doing my regular job for Brittany. Heidi barely did anything. I don't know what came over me. I just snapped."

Angie looked quickly behind her. There had to be another way out. "And that's why you hit her with a flower vase."

"How do you know that?" Cheryl asked, her voice rising. "I was very careful putting back the arrangement."

Angie held her hands up. "You did a great job. Honest. And you did it when no one saw you. How is that possible? I admit that those strippers were distracting, but…"

"No one notices me," Cheryl said sadly. "Not even Brittany. I'm the assistant. Invisibility is my superpower."

"Are you kidding? You are an essential part of the team. This wedding wouldn't have happened without you."

"Oh, sure," Cheryl muttered as she took the last stone steps. "I'm noticeable when something goes wrong. Then everyone is looking for me."

"What's wrong with being invisible?" Angie asked. "It's comfortable. It's safe. It means you're doing something right."

"Oh, what would you know about being invisible?" she spat out. "That stripper picked you out of a crowd of women. Beautiful, glamorous women who know the difference between Prada and Pucci. And he can't keep his eyes off you."

"Brittany notices what you do. She's desperately looking for you now." Angie glanced at the small church building. What was taking Robin so long?

"And when she finds me, I will be tending to your concussion," she said sweetly as she advanced. "Everyone knows you can't walk in heels."

"That may have worked before but not this time," Angie said as she scurried back. She jumped when the prickly needles from the hedge poked her behind. "You let everyone think Heidi had too much to drink. But you didn't know that Heidi was clean and sober."

"I don't believe you. Brittany talked constantly about Heidi's wild antics. I knew the woman was going to be trouble before I met her."

"And when Heidi was out, you saw this as your chance to get into the wedding. You wanted to be a bridesmaid." Angie shook her head with disbelief. "Why?"

"Why? A bridesmaid is chosen based on how close she is to the bride. Someone who is important and part of the bride's life. Brittany hasn't seen Heidi and Robin for years. They didn't know what was going on in Brittany's life. I do. I'm with Brittany every day. I'm an important part of her life."

"I'm sure—"

"Do you know why Brittany became a personal shopper?" Cheryl asked. "Or what her goals and dreams are? Do you know what problems she had to overcome to get where she is today? I do."

"So what?" Angie said, shrugging. "I could find all that out if I wanted to. Brittany doesn't strike me as a very private person."

"*So what?* I know every intimate detail of Brittany's life. I am her closest confidante. I get rid of obstacles in her life and I protect her. I should have been a bridesmaid." Cheryl flattened her hand on her chest. "I should have been picked to be the maid of honor."

"You've definitely proven how indispensible you are in Brittany's life. If she didn't know it before, she definitely knows it now."

"She appreciates me," Cheryl shouted. "I know she does."

Angie cringed. Her instincts were to duck and take cover, but she had to keep her talking. She had to buy herself more time. "But you did your job too well," Angie decided. "She wanted you to stay in your role of assistant and she made Robin maid of honor."

"I know. I couldn't believe it." Her face twisted with anger. "Robin? Robin was worse than Heidi."

"So how did you get rid of her?" Angie asked. "You put something in her drink, didn't you?"

Cheryl suddenly stopped advancing. She took a step back and gave Angie an assessing stare.

"Oh, come on," Angie said with a tentative smile. "You know I have no proof. You got rid of the martini glass the minute Robin started to show symptoms."

"How long have you known that it was me?" Cheryl looked at her as if she were a new type of threat.

"I didn't," she admitted. But she wouldn't dare mention Cole's observations or how he had been investigating the accident. "I thought Robin hurt Heidi because she deserves the maid-of-honor role."

"Deserves? Are you kidding?" Cheryl's voice overpowered the organ music coming from the church. "Robin didn't deserve it at all. All she cared about was getting lucky at the wedding. Like being the maid of honor would give her the extra edge. Right. A little peanut oil in the martini took care of that."

Angie was amazed at Cheryl's blaze attitude. "You could have killed her."

Cheryl snorted at the suggestion. "Why do you think I asked you to look for her? You and your stripper boyfriend had jumped into action at the bachelorette party. I knew you'd find her."

"And you got me kicked out of the wedding."

Cheryl laughed. "I'm good, but I'm not that good. That was a stroke of luck and I thought I had finally protected Brittany's dream wedding. This was my chance to be the bridesmaid. It was my reward. I could be part of Brittany's special day. Everything was working in my favor." She frowned. "But Patrick talked Brittany into letting you back in the wedding."

"And now you're after me. Why?" Angie asked. She took a step to the side and was no longer trapped between the hedges and Cheryl. "Why don't you take out Robin? She's weak."

"She's extra cautious now. Not to mention everyone is fussing over her all the time. Also, Brittany wanted Robin in the wedding."

"And Brittany doesn't want me here," Angie concluded. The bride would be happy to have her out of the wedding and thus be more willing to add her assistant in at the last minute.

"Exactly." Cheryl's smile sent chills down Angie's spine. "She doesn't want you anywhere in her life. Expect to slowly fade from Patrick's social circle."

"I can't believe you did all this to be a bridesmaid." She pressed her hand against her head and discovered that half of her updo was falling out. She blew a chunk of hair out of her eyes. "It's a horrible job."

"I'm doing this because I care about Brittany," Cheryl argued. "I got rid of all of the fake friends and backstabbing bridesmaids. Brittany deserves to be surrounded by people who actually love and adore her."

"You have a strange way of showing friendship. And, honestly, being a bridesmaid is a test of will and patience. Think about it," Angie stressed as she took another side step. "You have to be at the bride's beck and call. You have to put your life on hold and put up with the bride's rages. Do you have any idea what that feels like? Oh, wait. Maybe you do."

"But this way everyone will know that I'm more than her employee," Cheryl said, raising her voice. "I'm her friend."

"No, she will never think that." Angie was reluctant to share this with Cheryl, but the woman had to know that Brittany would never see her as an equal. "Brittany said so herself. When the suggestion was made to replace you for Heidi, Brittany made it very clear that you were only the assistant."

"She wouldn't say that!" Cheryl shouted. "Brittany likes me. She likes me more than any of her bridesmaids."

Angie took another step. She was almost in the clear to make a run for the stone steps. "Even if you did get rid of me, she won't add you to the ceremony."

"Yes, she will." Cheryl grabbed her arm and squeezed tight. "She'll be in a panic and she'll want me right there."

"Fine." She tried to shake off Cheryl's hold but it was no use. "You know what? You don't need to take me out of commission. You want to take my place? Go for it."

Cheryl looked at her as if she sensed a trick. "You're not going to fight it?"

"I'll be relieved. I didn't want to do this, anyway. Tell

Brittany that I twisted my ankle while I was looking for you. She won't want me hobbling down the aisle."

"True." She tightened her hold on Angie's arm. "But how do I know you won't talk?"

Angie wasn't sure if she could come up with a convincing reason not to. "You said it yourself. There is no proof. Everything you used is gone." When Cheryl nodded, Angie kept going. "It's just my word against yours. And everyone thinks I'll say anything to ruin the wedding."

"I'm glad we're in agreement. Okay, I'll take your place." She pointed at Angie's other arm. "Now hand over the bracelet."

Angie curled her hand closer to her body. "Why?"

"Brittany gave it to her bridesmaids as a gift during the bridesmaids' luncheon," Cheryl said. "I was there. I picked out the bracelet. Why shouldn't I get one?"

"You shouldn't get one because you weren't a bridesmaid," Angie muttered as an idea formed in her head.

"But I am now." She held out her other hand. "Give it to me."

Angie slid the bracelet from her wrist and threw it as Cheryl reached for it.

"What are you doing?" Cheryl asked as she watched the bracelet fall into the dirt.

Angie swung her foot out and swiped Cheryl's legs from underneath her. They both fell down. "Cheryl," she said as they wrestled for control. "I don't care about being a bridesmaid, but no one tries to hurt me and gets away with it."

COLE SAT IN the back of the church and glanced at his watch. The wedding should have already started. What was taking so long?

He looked at the entrance where the procession should be. Instead, he saw only Robin hovering by the door. She seemed worried, almost frantic, as she motioned for him to meet her in the hallway.

Cole quickly followed her. "What's going on, Robin?"

"Have you seen Angie?" she whispered.

Her words were like a kick to his system. His body was on full alert and he immediately checked his phone. "Not since you saw me with her. Why?"

"This isn't good." Robin began chewing on her fingernail. "I've checked every room and closet hoping she was with you."

"How long has it been since you've seen her?"

"I don't know. It feels like forever," Robin admitted as tears shone in her eyes. "Brittany was freaking out and I couldn't get a hold of Cheryl on my phone. Angie went to look for her and now they're both missing."

"Keep searching inside the church. I'll go outside." He broke into a run and looked around the front steps. He didn't see anyone. He thought of the parking lot and then the church grounds. His instinct was to head for the grounds.

He ran to the side of the church, calling out Angie's name. He saw a thick wall of hedges and was about to go around them when he heard the sound of a struggle. "Angie?"

"Cole?" Angie called out. "I'm in the garden— Ow!"

Cole pushed his way through the thick shrubbery. It felt like it took him ages as he slapped, kicked and clawed his way in. He had to get to Angie. He would never forgive himself if something happened to her.

He heard Angie's scream and the sound of a body slamming against the ground. His heart twisted with fear. Cole let out a roar as he crashed through the last of the shrubbery and found Angie wrestling on the grass with Cheryl.

Angie struggled as she rolled back and forth with Cheryl. Her hair was flying out of her bun and a long grass stain streaked down her dress. Dirt and scratches covered her arms, legs and chest.

He rushed forward but Angie had staggered to her feet and was pointing at Cheryl. "Don't you dare move," she told the assistant, who lay limp and moaning.

"Need some help?" Cole asked as he wrapped his arm around Angie's waist. He peered into her eyes and frowned when he saw a bruise forming under one of them.

"You can call your friend, that woman who was the first police officer at the strip club. Cheryl confessed to injuring Heidi and Robin."

"You don't have any proof," Cheryl said weakly.

"You were also seen in a physical altercation with Angie," Cole said, refusing to look at Cheryl. "And you have me as a witness."

Cheryl made a face as if dismissing his claim. "Who's going to listen to a stripper?"

"Hey." Angie bumped Cheryl's hip with her shoe. "His name is Cole Foster and he's a private investigator and a former cop."

"What?" Cheryl said in a squawk. "Brittany didn't say anything about this."

Angie shook her head. "You've really got to stop using Brittany as your only source of information."

Cole saw something gold glitter in the dirt. He bent down and picked up a thin bracelet.

"That's mine," Angie said, extending her hand.

Cole held her fingers gently and slid it onto her wrist. "How did you lose this in a fight?"

"Cheryl tried to take it." She held up her wrist and let the sunshine gleam off the gold. "She thought she should have it."

"You said I could be a bridesmaid," Cheryl wailed.

"Cheryl, I may be just a close friend of the groom's and I may have a bad attitude toward weddings, but I'm wearing this bracelet because I earned it." She lowered her hand. "But don't worry, Cheryl. You're going to get a pair of metal, police-issued ones. You definitely earned those."

19

"I CAN'T BELIEVE Brittany kicked you out of the wedding again," Cole said as he carried Angie into her apartment. "After all you did for her."

"I don't mind," said Angie as she lifted her arm and allowed the bracelet to sparkle under the hallway light. "I still got a bracelet out of this deal."

"And least this time Tim and Steven argued on your behalf," he stated, shutting the door behind them. "I thought they were going to go slide in the mud in solidarity with you."

Angie smiled. "I think they wanted to blow off some steam. It had nothing to do with me."

Cole wasn't so sure. He knew Angie's friends were impressed by her taking down Cheryl and finding out the real reason behind the accidents. They were very vocal in their displeasure when Brittany refused to have Angie continue being a bridesmaid based on her scruffy appearance.

"Cole, you can put me down now," Angie told him as he brushed past the sofa and went straight to the bed.

"My ankle is just twisted. And that wasn't from Cheryl. That was from hurrying in these heels."

"Obviously the only safe place for you to wear these shoes is in bed with me." He laid her down. He took off his jacket and wrenched off his tie. Cole felt the anger and fear roll through him again as he cupped her jaw and studied her scratched-up face. "That is some black eye."

She shrugged. "It'll heal."

He caressed her cheek. "I never should have left you alone in the church. I knew Cheryl was behind all this. I knew she was out to get you."

"Don't blame yourself, please. We had no proof. And I had everything under control. But I was glad I had you as backup."

"I will always be there for you." He leaned down and kissed her gently. "I, too, argued to keep you in the wedding."

"Oh, I heard. The whole church heard. At least I got to see Patrick get married. That's all I really wanted." She pulled at the frayed hem of her dress. "The minute I saw these stains down the front of me, I knew there was no way Brittany would let me walk down the aisle."

Cole couldn't believe the bride's ingratitude. "Like I said, after all you did for her."

"I know, right?" Angie's eyes twinkled. "It's okay. I saved the day and the wedding went on. Patrick knows I did it for him. And I uncovered how crazy Cheryl really is. I wonder what will happen to her."

"She was saying a lot when they took her away." Cheryl's excuses and explanations were not going to help her case.

"She felt invisible because the most important person in her life didn't share her feelings. I thought I understood how she felt but I was wrong. You see me, even when I try to hide."

"It's pointless to hide from me."

"It is," Angie agreed as she pulled Cole down on top of her.

"Angie," he warned as she rolled over so she was on top. "Forget it. You need to rest."

"Later," she promised as she placed a sweet kiss on his lips. "Right now, I need to be with you."

And he needed to be with her. He realized that days ago but had been slow to act on it. Her pseudo-accident changed that.

"Angie, when I was trying to get to you, I had this one thought going through my mind the whole time." He felt almost queasy as he remembered the bitter taste of fear. "I was worried that if something happened, I would never have the chance to tell you that I love you."

He felt the tension in Angie's body before she lifted her head and looked into his eyes. "Now's your chance."

He frowned. "Weren't you listening? I just did."

"Cole," urged Angie, "tell me exactly how you feel."

Cole didn't feel nervous as he held her gaze. He wanted her to know. He wanted the world to know how he felt about this woman. "I love you, Angie. At first I thought it made me weak. Vulnerable. I didn't want to show how much you meant to me because I would give you power over me."

"What changed?"

"You've always had power over me, whether or not I told you how I feel. From the second I met you. But you didn't use it against me."

"Cole, I'm going to let you in on a little secret." She

leaned forward until her mouth was a kiss away from his. "I'm not powerful but you make me feel that way. Like right now. I'm excited and anxious. I feel safe but adventurous. When you look at me like that, I want to be everything to you."

"You are," he insisted. "And I was lost and miserable after I left you. I believed I was doing the right thing but I wished every day that I hadn't ended things. And it was a mistake that I waited so long to see you again."

"I won't lie, Cole, it hurt when you took off," she said, her eyes darkening as she recalled the pain. "I tried to get over you but I couldn't."

"Yeah, I remember your face when you saw me on stage." She had been confused and angry. It gave him a little bit of hope that she still had feelings for him.

Angie sat up straight and tightened her legs around his hips. "That reminds me, no more undercover work, especially in a strip club."

"Don't worry. I'm never doing that again." The only woman he wanted tearing his clothes off was Angie. "The one good thing that came out of that is that you owe me a lap dance."

Her mouth dropped open. "Says who?"

He moved restlessly underneath her as he imagined her performance wearing nothing but those impractical heels. "Come on, Angie. Let me watch you."

She hesitated as if she were actually considering his suggestion. "How much cash do you have?"

"That depends," he said as his gaze traveled down her body. "What are you offering to do?"

ANGIE SUDDENLY FELT shy. Shy, but intrigued. She nervously licked her lips. "There's no music."

"Doesn't matter." His voice sounded gravelly as

she saw the lust sharpen his features. "I just want to watch you."

Angie liked the idea but it would be so revealing. She wanted to seduce Cole and make him go wild underneath her. Show him how she felt. Get pleasure from his pleasure. She wanted to be as bold as she used to be.

But she wanted him to do more than just watch. "Guide me through it."

"You don't need any help," he said with a smile. Slowly, he slid his hands under his head and shifted to find a comfortable spot on the bed. "Go for it."

Angie stared at him and her heart did a strange little flip. His rumpled white shirt was pulled tight against his broad chest. His position was almost casual, but his expression was serious. He was giving her all the power. And showing her he was open to anything, while still encouraging her. She could do whatever she wanted and he would enjoy the ride.

She tentatively rolled her hips for him and then raised her short skirt. The fabric was slick and silky against her bare legs. She ran her hands along her thighs, imagining how Cole would often touch her that way when he was overcome with desire. She splayed her fingers over her breasts before skimming them along her throat and cheeks.

"Stop teasing," Cole said hoarsely. "Give me all you got."

She smiled and dragged down his zipper, then pulled his belt free. "Take off your clothes," she requested.

Cole did so, his actions quick and impatient. When his underwear hit the floor, he settled back on the bed, his penis thick and proudly erect. Heavy anticipation crashed through Angie as she grasped the base of his cock. Cole hissed between clenched teeth and bucked into her hand.

Angie bit her lip as she watched Cole's reaction. Yes, she was giving him pleasure, but he was giving her his trust. Cole was tough, he could take control again any time he wanted, but what he wanted was for her to have it.

"Take off your dress," he said, mimicking her earlier request of him. "Keep the shoes on." He grinned playfully.

Angie reached behind her. She couldn't wait to lie with Cole, skin on skin. "I need your help."

Cole rose and sat up. Angie watched him intensely, her sex clenching as her peaked nipples rasped against the tight material. She couldn't hide her shiver as Cole lowered the zipper. His hands were large and strong against the simple, fragile dress. She wanted him to rip off the fabric. Instead he peeled it off her gradually. She stretched, exaggerating each move as the intense arousal soared through her. She arched her back and thrust her breasts.

Once he removed her dress, Angie slowly exhaled, her breath echoing in the charged silence. She laid her hands on Cole's shoulders, her fingers digging into his muscles. She could feel his hot gaze on her breasts. Her skin tingled as Cole licked his lips. She waited for him to take her into his mouth.

"Keep dancing, Angie. Show off your body."

Angie held back a frustrated cry. Dancing wasn't on her mind. There was no music, except for the thrumming beat of her heart. His mouth was right at the tips of her breasts. She wanted to feel his tongue on her. She wanted him to tease her everywhere until she was begging for mercy.

She would have *him* begging for mercy, she decided. Angie caught his eye and fondled her breasts, moaning from the unreal pleasure. She felt Cole's burning passion when she gasped while pinching her nipples. She pinched harder, tilting her head back and calling out his name.

Angie slid her hands down her flat stomach before cupping her sex. She held his gaze. She no longer felt shy. She felt powerful. Naughty. Demanding. She dipped one hand into her panties and stroked the slick folds of her sex.

Cole drew her hands to her sides and held her hips. He slid something cold and metallic along her skin. She looked down and stilled. "I-is that…"

"This is the key to my apartment," he said softly. "I want you to have it."

She stared at the silver key chain. It was simple and elegant with just one key. He had made a key for her. And bought the key chain with her in mind. Excitement pulsed through her, but she was afraid she was misreading his gesture. "Why?" she asked and caution fought with elation.

"I want you to move in with me." His voice was a whisper as he stripped her panties down her legs. The key chain slipped from his fingers and fell on the bed.

"Are you sure?" she asked, helping him remove the last item of clothing. Her legs wobbled as she straddled him again. She didn't want to push him into anything.

"Yes, this is just the beginning," he said as he placed his hands on her hips and guided her down. "One of these days I'm going to convince you to marry me."

Angie groaned as Cole stretched and filled her. His words reverberated in her head. She leaned into him, sinking deeper as she wrapped her arms around his shoulders.

"I'm all for marriage," Angie said as she vibrated with need. "I said I wasn't going to marry. But that was because I thought you didn't want marriage."

Cole threaded his fingers through her hair and held her tight. She couldn't look away from him even if she wanted to. "I'm going to marry you, Angie."

"Yes." She rocked forward and back, setting a wild pace, chasing the pleasure. Cole held on to her, surging against her pressing hips. His thrusts were hard, relentless until he found his release. He kept her tightly in his arms as he pulsed into her and she climaxed.

Cole fell back onto the bed, taking Angie with him. She sank against Cole as she tried to catch her breath. The blood pounded in her ears and her heart beat against her ribs. Her skin was hot and sticky with sweat but she didn't want to move. She could stay curled against Cole forever.

"I'm going to ask you again," Cole said roughly as he held her beside him. She noticed his hand trembled as he stroked her damp hair. "I don't want you to think I said it in the heat of the moment."

"The answer will always be the same," Angie said before she kissed his neck, his cheek and mouth. "Today, tomorrow, or on our golden anniversary. I love you, Cole. And the answer will always be yes."

Epilogue

BEST. BACHELORETTE. PARTY. EVER. Angie whooped with delight at the thought. She pumped her hands up in the air as she watched the men posture and swing their sticks for the crowd. Despite their thick and powerful legs, these men were agile. Poetry in motion. She couldn't tear her gaze away.

"Angie, what are you doing?" Brittany asked with a sigh of disapproval.

"Having the time of my life," Angie replied, staring at the macho display in front of her. "Are you still having trouble understanding what's going on? Do you want me to explain it to you again?"

"No, once was enough," Brittany declared. "But this is supposed to be your bachelorette party. We should be staring at strippers instead of hockey players."

Angie disagreed. She rarely got the chance to watch the local hockey team play and this was the first time she'd attended the game in the comfort of the sky box. It offered her the best view of the action.

"I don't need strippers," Angie told Brittany as she bit back a naughty smile. "I have my own at home."

"Spare me the details. I don't want to know. But you should realize that you broke the golden rule for bachelorette parties. You invited the guys!" She gestured at the window, where Patrick and Cole cheered loudly for their team.

"I wanted all my friends here." Angie paid attention to the goalie defending the net with a blocked shot. She cheered and looked around the sky box. Tim and Steven were flirting with every unattached woman at the party and her brothers were enjoying the game with their girlfriends. It had taken a while before her brothers and her basketball buddies accepted Cole, but now they'd gladly given their collective blessing since they could see how happy he made her. Next week at this time her friends and family would be present when she married Cole in a casual yet intimate wedding.

Brittany picked at the hem of Angie's oversize hockey jersey and shook her head. "Couldn't you have at least worn a tiara?"

"I don't need to." She waved her ring finger in front of the woman's face. "I have all the glitter I need."

Brittany grasped Angie's finger and studied the engagement ring. She clucked her tongue at the lack of manicure but lowered her head in defeat. "Okay, I admit Cole did well in choosing diamonds."

"No, Brittany," Cole said, slipping his arm around Angie's waist and gathering her close. "I did well in choosing a bride."

"Oh, please," Brittany lamented as she watched Cole capture Angie's earlobe with the edge of his teeth. "Can you save that for the honeymoon?"

"I can't help it," Angie said as she turned and looked

up at Cole. She cupped his cheek with her hand and his features softened. Her breath caught in her throat when she saw the love and desire in his eyes. "When I'm with Cole, there's no holding back."

* * * * *

Available October 22, 2013

#771 BACK IN SERVICE
Uniformly Hot!
by Isabel Sharpe
The girl whom injured airman Jameson Cartwright teased mercilessly in grade school has grown into a sexy, fun, vibrant woman. Kendra Lonergan wants to help him recover; he just wants her...in his bed!

#772 NO DESIRE DENIED
Forbidden Fantasies
by Cara Summers
Children's author Nell MacPherson has always had an active imagination. And with a stalker on her tail and sexy Secret Service agent Reid Sutherland in her bed, she's finding a whole new world of inspiration—the X-rated kind!

#773 DRIVING HER WILD
by Meg Maguire
When she retires from the ring, MMA fighter Steph Healy thinks she's left her toughest opponents behind her. Little does she know, a hapless, hot-blooded contractor will bring her to her knees....

#774 HER LAST BEST FLING
by Candace Havens
Macy Reynolds is looking for her big break, and she's hoping a scoop featuring Blake Michaels, the town's returning hero, will give it to her. Unfortunately, the hot marine has no intention of telling the sexy little newspaper publisher anything. But he'll *show* her....

REQUEST YOUR FREE BOOKS!
2 FREE NOVELS PLUS 2 FREE GIFTS!

red-hot reads!

YES! Please send me 2 FREE Harlequin® Blaze™ novels and my 2 FREE gifts (gifts are worth about $10). After receiving them, if I don't wish to receive any more books, I can return the shipping statement marked "cancel." If I don't cancel, I will receive 4 brand-new novels every month and be billed just $4.49 per book in the U.S. or $4.96 per book in Canada. That's a savings of at least 14% off the cover price. It's quite a bargain. Shipping and handling is just 50¢ per book in the U.S. and 75¢ per book in Canada.* I understand that accepting the 2 free books and gifts places me under no obligation to buy anything. I can always return a shipment and cancel at any time. Even if I never buy another book, the two free books and gifts are mine to keep forever.

150/350 HDN FV42

Name	(PLEASE PRINT)	
Address		Apt. #
City	State/Prov.	Zip/Postal Code

Signature (if under 18, a parent or guardian must sign)

Mail to the **Harlequin® Reader Service:**
IN U.S.A.: P.O. Box 1867, Buffalo, NY 14240-1867
IN CANADA: P.O. Box 609, Fort Erie, Ontario L2A 5X3

Want to try two free books from another line?
Call 1-800-873-8635 or visit www.ReaderService.com.

* Terms and prices subject to change without notice. Prices do not include applicable taxes. Sales tax applicable in N.Y. Canadian residents will be charged applicable taxes. Offer not valid in Quebec. This offer is limited to one order per household. Not valid for current subscribers to Harlequin Blaze books. All orders subject to credit approval. Credit or debit balances in a customer's account(s) may be offset by any other outstanding balance owed by or to the customer. Please allow 4 to 6 weeks for delivery. Offer available while quantities last.

Your Privacy—The Harlequin® Reader Service is committed to protecting your privacy. Our Privacy Policy is available online at www.ReaderService.com or upon request from the Harlequin Reader Service.

We make a portion of our mailing list available to reputable third parties that offer products we believe may interest you. If you prefer that we not exchange your name with third parties, or if you wish to clarify or modify your communication preferences, please visit us at www.ReaderService.com/consumerschoice or write to us at Harlequin Reader Service Preference Service, P.O. Box 9062, Buffalo, NY 14269. Include your complete name and address.

No Desire Denied

"In one of my books, this would be a plot point. The characters would have to make a decision. Either they find out and deal with the consequences or they keep thinking about it. I would assume that in your job, it pays to know exactly what you're up against. Right?"

"Close enough."

But *he* wasn't nearly close enough. The heat of his breath burned her lips, but she had to have more. And talking wasn't going to get it for her. If she wanted to seduce Reid, *she* had to make the move.

Finally her arms were around him, her mouth parted beneath his. And she had her answers.

His mouth wasn't soft at all, but open and urgent. His taste was as dark and dangerous as the man. That much she'd guessed. But there was none of the control that he always seemed to coat himself with. None of the reserve. There was only heat and luxurious demand. She was sinking fast to a place where there was nothing but Reid and the glorious sensations only he could give her. She wanted to lose herself in them. Her heart had never raced this fast. Her body had never pulsed so desperately. Even in her wildest fantasies, she'd never conceived of feeling this way. And it still wasn't enough. She needed more. Everything. Him. Digging her fingers into his shoulders, she pulled him closer.

Big mistake.

In some far corner of Reid's mind, the words blinked like a huge neon sign. They'd started sending their message the instant he'd told her they would settle what was happening between them now. He'd gotten out of the car to gain some distance, some perspective. Some resolve. But the brief respite had only seemed to increase the seductive pull Nell had on him.

He'd been a goner the moment he'd stuffed himself back into the front seat.

Long before that.

Oh, her argument had been flawless. Knowing exactly what you were up against was key in his job. Reid heartily wished it was her logic that had made his hands streak into her hair and not the feelings that she'd been arousing in him all day.

For seven years.

The hunger she'd triggered while she'd been talking so logically felt as if it had been buried inside him forever. Then once her lips pressed against his, he forgot everything except that he was finally kissing her. Finally touching her hair. He hadn't imagined how silky the texture would be. One hand remained there, trapped, while the other roamed freely, moving down and over her, memorizing the curves and angles in one possessive stroke.

Pick up NO DESIRE DENIED by Cara Summers, available October 22, 2013, wherever you buy Harlequin® Blaze® books.

HBEXP79776

Recovery...one hot night at a time!

It was the cat's fault. Otherwise
Jameson Cartwright wouldn't have tripped and
ruined not only his knee, but also his newly minted
air force career and the Cartwright family pride.
Now he's lying low and miserable—until the girl he
tormented as a kid comes breezing through his
door, looking fresh and sexy. This time, it's *his* turn
to be exquisitely and thoroughly tortured....

Pick up

Back in Service

by *Isabel Sharpe,*
available October 22, 2013, wherever you buy
Harlequin Blaze books.

Red-Hot Reads
www.Harlequin.com